HEATHER BOYD

USA TODAY BESTSELLING AUTHOR

Naughty and Nice

Love Me Tender

Naughty and Nice Series in print

One Wicked Night and other short stories
In the Widow's Bed
Love Me Tender
Love Me True
A Husband for Mary
Let It Snow

DEDICATION

To freedom.

CHAPTER ONE

July, 1814
Devizes, Wiltshire

THE SLEEPY AFTERNOON silence of the Davey Lending Library ended abruptly with the harsh jangle of the doorbell and rushed footsteps crossing the room. Winifred Moore turned from the bookshelf she was filling with new books in time to glimpse a dark shape disappearing behind the bookshop counter.

Fearing a thief had designs on the day's meager takings, Winifred hurried to protect her father's business interests, holding a tome before her as a weapon.

"Please, pretend I'm not here," a deep, masculine voice rumbled up from the vicinity of the floor. "I shall inconvenience you just a few moments."

Winifred rounded the corner of the counter and spied a dandy lying on the shop floor. Quite unused to such a dubious honor, the widow took a moment to memorize the image for her later fantasies. Dark, windswept hair, greatcoat open to expose the expensive tailoring of his superior class. Matching sapphire cravat pin and signet ring identified the owner of the piercing, blue eyes as the favorite son of the Duke of Devizes. His heir.

Winifred stepped back. "My lord, you should not be upon our floor."

Tristan Greene, Viscount Ramsbury, propped himself on one elbow and flashed a cheeky grin. "My dear Mrs. Moore, I am exactly where I wish to be."

Winifred glanced at the dusty floor, sorely in need of sweeping after a long day of business, and shuddered. "Have a care for your consequence, Lord Ramsbury, or you risk becoming quite unpresentable."

The viscount laughed. "If I am indeed in Mr. Davey's Lending Library on High Street, then my consequence will be utterly preserved."

Winifred glanced toward the door,

longing for her father's early return from his book-buying trip to Bristol, or any other timely interruption that would banish this foolish delusion. After several moments, when no parental guidance or visiting custom intruded, she pinched her hand to return to sanity. Unfortunately, Viscount Ramsbury still adorned her dusty floor. Only one logical explanation occurred to her. "Are you foxed, my lord?"

Ramsbury straightened his greatcoat about his legs. "Oh, would that I were, but during times such as these a man must keep a level head upon his shoulders else he'll run afoul of a fiendish plot."

Winifred slid her book to the table. "Are you in danger, Lord Ramsbury?"

"Danger of the most perilous kind," he murmured, glancing about him unconcerned. "But the shelter of your premises is the most perfect foxhole a desperate man can hope to find. I am most grateful to you."

Clearly, the viscount had lied about his consumption of spirits. "Grateful?"

Ramsbury flashed another smile she felt all the way to her toes. A warm flush swept over her skin as his gaze skimmed down her body. Then, he tipped his head toward the front of the shop. "Yes, grateful that Miss Claribel Wheaton prefers not to read."

Puzzled, Winifred glanced out the window and spied Miss Wheaton across the road. The young woman seemed most comical today, peering into all the Devizes's shop windows with great enthusiasm, dragging her companion forward by the arm. Suddenly, a whisper Winifred had overheard and had discounted as ridiculous gossip explained the viscount's actions.

She smiled. "I believe I begin to understand your dilemma, my lord." Winifred chuckled, and then quickly suppressed the unkind thoughts swirling through her mind about Miss Wheaton's designs to become the next Lady Ramsbury. "Indeed you are quite correct in your assessment of your safety. Miss Wheaton does not visit the lending library often."

The viscount sat up. "Do you mean to say she does come into this establishment?"

"Only when forced to by a visiting relation. At present, I believe she is without the company of her extended family."

The viscount subsided to the floor, crossed his ankles, then tucked his hands behind his head as if he planned to be there awhile. "I'd be much obliged if you could inform me when

Miss Wheaton's coach departs. I believe the conveyance stands at the ready beside the seamstress' establishment."

Winifred approached the window. As Lord Ramsbury suggested, Miss Wheaton's carriage awaited her and her companion some distance away. The lady in question, however, had reached the last business on the street and after a short debate with her companion crossed the road. "The enemy advances, my lord," Winifred warned. "Have a care for your continued freedom."

Behind her, Lord Ramsbury moved—a rush of footsteps across the floor, the rear door crashed shut, and the lending library fell silent again. Winifred returned to the counter and picked up her book, disappointed the unusual disturbance had passed so quickly. But with luck, Lord Ramsbury would be halfway home by the time Miss Wheaton returned to her carriage.

The doorbell jangled again. When she turned, she found Miss Wheaton edging into the shop.

"Miss Wheaton, what a delightful surprise!" Winifred exclaimed, hurrying forward with the intention of drawing the young woman farther into the shop. If possible, she could entice her to use the lending library's services, make her father happy with the added custom, and ensure Lord Ramsbury got away cleanly.

"Mrs. Moore," Miss Wheaton answered, but didn't budge from the door's arch. "Are you unwell? Your face is unfashionably flushed. Quite an unfortunate shade of pink, truth to tell."

Could Winifred ever stop her emotions from sweeping across her skin? Probably not. The telltale flush always gave her away. Usually, she'd ignore the disparaging remark, but to hear Miss Wheaton comment upon Winifred's unpopular looks, especially after her brief encounter with the handsome viscount, infuriated her.

"I always enjoy excellent health, Miss Wheaton. But I am gratified to see you recovered from your recent indisposition."

The young woman sighed dramatically. "You wouldn't know from your limited acquaintance with the Duchess of Devizes, but boating upon the river in her company is an exhilarating, albeit exhausting, undertaking. I defy anyone to endure it without fatigue."

Winifred hadn't been invited to the picnic or to go boating, much to her disappointment.

But she shouldn't be cast down by her exclusion. Her black widow's weeds would have dampened the festive mood of the duchess's gathering. And it wasn't proper for a widow to display too much enjoyment, especially so early in her period of mourning. Winifred squared her shoulders, determined not to let Devizes's reigning debutante get any farther under her skin. At least she had been married. "How may I be of service, Miss Wheaton? Were you looking for a particular book?"

Miss Wheaton wrinkled her nose, as though an unpleasant smell had reached her. "No, thank you, Mrs. Moore. I merely stopped to be polite. I cannot abide how you appeared to be hanging out the window in search of new customers. Quite unseemly. Good day to you."

"Good day"—the door rattled shut—"Miss Wheaton."

Of all the rude, cruel creatures to walk Devizes's streets, Miss Wheaton behaved the worst. Winifred glanced at the clock, and, seeing only minutes remained until closing time, she locked the front door, then drew the drapes over the front windows. Privacy and a long night of blissful solitude lay ahead. Tonight, she could be herself.

"Is she like that all the time, so puffed up

with her own sense of self worth that she thinks she can scold you?"

Winifred yelped and turned around. Across the room, leaning idly against the door leading to the family's private rooms, stood the viscount, watching her. "My lord, you scared me. I thought you'd gone."

"Not yet." Ramsbury stepped forward, skirting the shop counter until his greatcoat brushed her gown. "I asked a question. Is she rude to you on a regular basis?"

Winifred's skin heated to match her embarrassment. She dropped her gaze to his cravat pin, unprepared to be honest about the snubs she'd endured since her return.

The viscount caught her chin and raised her face until she met his bright blue gaze. "Jealousy truly does bring out the worst in women, doesn't it?"

Winifred tried to hold Ramsbury's direct stare but found it impossible. He was, quite possibly, the most sought after and admired man in three districts, but he was also her social superior. Allowing him liberties, however minor, would only diminish her remaining reputation. "I cannot imagine what you mean."

She stepped back, feeling the slide of firm, bare skin caress her chin.

"They're all a bunch of spiteful tabbies," he murmured, following her retreat. "Could you ever imagine your return to Devizes would be responsible for the salvation of Mrs. Lynch's business? I'm told she's quite worn out from the rush."

Although Winifred hadn't caught the scent of strong spirits on Ramsbury's breath, he must be deep in his cups to speak as he did. "How could I be responsible for the dressmaker's exhaustion? I haven't purchased a new gown in an age."

Lord Ramsbury smiled, a wicked flash of teeth that set her heart to thumping. He slid closer, forcing her tight against the counter. Winifred drew a cautious breath but still detected nothing to account for his addled state.

"Because every single man in three districts has heard of your return and, like me, waits for brief glimpses of you outside these walls. The unmarried ladies are poised on every corner to tempt us in your absence but few spare them any attention. Do you never go out?"

Winifred's heart pounded, from the compliment and from the touch of the viscount's fingers over her arm. Did he have to stand so close?

"My father likes to keep me busy." Winifred gulped. "I am in mourning, after all."

The viscount eased backward an inch. "You were only married a month. Will you mourn him the full year?"

No one had ever dared to ask her how she felt about her widowed state. No one expected her to be happier as a widow than she had been as a wife. The viscount's direct question pleased her, and she wished she could answer honestly without appearing gauche.

Ramsbury's lips twitched. "You want to say no, don't you? Between us—the opportunistic bastard doesn't deserve one second of mourning."

Winifred stared at his lips, struck by his nearness and curiosity over how he would kiss. "I hadn't considered the matter. His death was all so sudden."

"I wouldn't have you mourn him a day." He lowered his head, and the soft press of his lips against her own surprised her. She had come to expect aggression, possession, and little choice in the matter of kisses. What a difference the morals of a man made. Ramsbury brushed his lips over hers, sending delightful thrills through her body. Winifred swallowed nervously. But he persisted, dropping gentle kisses on her lips, nibbling at the soft flesh. To her considerable astonishment, Winifred responded in a way she had only imagined in her nighttime fantasies. Every sense she possessed sprang to life and obscured the world around her.

Despite the desire to be good, respectable, Winifred closed her eyes and pressed closer to the viscount. The warmth of his body penetrated her hideous, black gown. His hard body crowded yet didn't overwhelm. He held his emotions in check, restrained his passion without forcing himself upon her as her husband had done.

Suddenly, her lips were cold. The viscount had pulled back. "You taste the same."

Heat swept across Winifred's cheeks. "How could you remember that? The kiss you stole at the Winter Ball seems so long ago."

"Because." He caressed her burning skin. "Once tasted, your sweetness is something a man could never get enough of; he would always want more."

Ramsbury kissed her again, pulled her so close she touched every inch of him, discovered the effect she had over his body. His aroused state thrilled her, and she shut her eyes to enjoy him better. He ate at her mouth with neat, precise kisses, then he caught her lower lip with his and tugged. Her eyes flew open at the stunning sensation. Winifred had learned a few valuable truths since becoming a wife and widow. Society deemed Lord Ramsbury a rake and a much-sought-after bed partner, despite his benign appearance. Since she'd joined their ranks, the previously prissy widows of town whispered now, within her hearing, that it was said he did not simply toss up one's skirts and have his way, but devoted hours to worshiping his lover.

Winifred could stand to be worshipped.

Feeling altogether reckless, she aligned their hips and pressed her lips harder against his. Ramsbury's gasp thrilled her, and Winifred reveled in her newfound power. She nuzzled his lips enthusiastically, and he groaned around her kisses. His lower lip tempted her, so she captured it and subjected Ramsbury to the same delicious torture. She might never have the chance to experience passion with a man of his accomplished reputation, and she wanted to see what all the fuss was about. Winifred threaded her fingers into his hair, letting her actions convey her desires.

He hitched her from the floor and pressed her body to the wall, pinning her with his hips as surely as if he were already inside her. He teased the sensitive sides of her breasts with his fingertips. Winifred squirmed restlessly in his grip. She didn't know where to put her hands or her dangling feet, but she wished these delicious sensations would never end.

Ramsbury appeared ravenous. He clutched and released her breasts, sending spikes of throbbing pleasure to her core. She wriggled and slid her leg around his thigh as far as her gown would allow. The viscount didn't misunderstand her encouragement. He pressed his groin harder against her body, letting the firm ridge of his erection rub against a place that ached. Yet, all the while, he nibbled lightly on her lips, never taking away her ability to refuse, never demanding more than she wanted to give. Cool air swirled about her ankles as he raised her long skirts. He caressed her stockings as he pushed her skirts higher. When he touched bare skin, she gasped out loud, rocking her hips desperately into the hard ridge of him.

"Shh," he whispered against her lips, before he claimed them again.

Winifred clutched his shoulders, unable to believe she was but moments away from becoming the viscount's next lover. Never in her bravest fantasies had her imagination led her so far. But she wanted him. She wanted to discover what lay beyond this desperate ache. She yearned to explore every sensation.

When their lips parted, Ramsbury held her tight, his warm breath churning over her throat. "Too fast," he whispered.

Did he scold himself, or had she behaved with too much passion? Ramsbury released her leg, letting her skirts fall, and she landed on the floor with a thud. He did not, however, release her completely, and that reassured Winifred her behavior had not been vulgar or unwanted. He clutched her close, digging his fingertips firmly into her bottom. They swayed, and Winifred couldn't help but twine her arms about his neck to draw him into another kiss.

Ramsbury pressed his hands to the wall on either side of her head. He angled his, and the wet swipe of his tongue across her lips curled her toes in her slippers. He licked her mouth again, short strokes that had her opening for him. He invaded, explored, and taught her that she understood nothing of kissing.

She could have died from the ecstasy of his taste, from the warmth of his tongue, and from her overwhelming need to stay connected to him.

When their lips parted, Ramsbury chuckled at her whimper. "And here I worried my pursuit too speedy. Such passion." He curled a broad hand around her nape and held their heads together. The viscount's breath beat fast against her lips. "When does your father return?"

Winifred's mind whirled as he peppered her temple with more kisses. She could lie and tell him her father returned soon, and he'd be on his way in a trice, or she could let the evening unfold to see what delights the viscount's touch might bring.

"He returns tomorrow. Late." The truth rolled off her tongue easily, and she blushed again at how forward she sounded. So much for her intention to avoid indiscretions. She would fall headlong into an altogether scandalous affair without even trying to prevent it. One touch, one, two, ten delicious kisses from Lord Ramsay had completely muddled her mind.

The viscount pressed his lips harder to her skin, then he released her completely. He picked up a sack from the floor. "I brought supper."

She studied the oddly shaped sack she hadn't noticed before. "Supper, my lord?"

He chuckled. "Perhaps not as my mother might expect. It's simple bachelor fare, but enough to satisfy the two of us."

Winifred smoothed her hands over her gown, self conscious that she'd almost been ravished and disappointed now that she had not. "How did you know my father had left town?"

The viscount's devilish smile stole her breath. "I, ah, overheard his conversation with the farrier yesterday."

She stared at him. His visit was not the surprise she had first imagined. He had come with seduction firmly in mind, not escape from Miss Wheaton. Winifred couldn't decide whether to be flattered or offended.

Ramsbury strode through the shop, shrugging out of his greatcoat as he went, moving toward the kitchen with his lumpy sack. His tuneless whistle preceded a noisy clatter, then the pop of a bottle opening rang through the air. "Rather than have me ransack the kitchen," he called, "would you care to join me and find us some glasses?"

Winifred rushed in, dug two of her father's best wineglasses from the battered cupboard, placed them on the table at his side, and then hurried to lock the rear door.

"A good decision," Ramsbury observed as he handed over a glass. "I might not be the only man bent on seduction tonight, but I'm fortunate enough to be the first to arrive."

Winifred put her glass down on the table. "That doesn't sound the least bit complimentary, my lord."

He chuckled again. "My lord? Perhaps we could dispense with the formalities at long last. Tristan."

Every nerve ending sizzled as she repeated his given name. *Tristan.* The name she whispered to the dark of night.

"Winifred." He moved close again, so close she could see the ring of black around his blue eyes. "A beautiful name to match the woman. Welcome home."

She couldn't hide the burst of happiness his words created. Their lips connected once more. Desire and delight destroyed her efforts to control her emotions. She gripped his coat and held him close to her. Why should she deny herself the very thing her wedding had promised but failed to deliver? She could, if she was very daring enjoy an interlude with the viscount. She had heard that many widows took lovers with no lasting harm if they were discreet about it. So far, Tristan appeared willing to accommodate her greedy demands for pleasure. He strummed over her breast with one thumb, while he squeezed her bottom with his other hand. His touch shattered her remaining desire to be a good and cautious woman. Winifred didn't resist. She encouraged, provoked, and set her hands upon his broad chest to begin removing his clothes.

Tristan released her, snapped his coat from his shoulders, tossed it in a heap on the floor, and pulled her close again before setting his lips to her neck. As his tongue flicked over the hollow of her throat, Winifred arched her back. Her late husband, Mr. Peter Moore, had never affected her senses like this. Quite the opposite, in fact. She reached for the edges of Tristan's waistcoat and began unbuttoning him, until a loud knock forced them apart.

CHAPTER TWO

TRISTAN SPUN toward the rear door, untangling his limbs from Winifred's enticingly lush body as the knock repeated. He glanced about the chamber, but couldn't see anywhere to secret himself except directly behind the door.

He had no wish to embarrass her or cause a scandal that would ruin her reputation. The auburn-haired beauty's kiss tasted sweeter than any claret, finer than any feast, and wholly unwise for a man committed to a bachelor existence. He'd noted her allure before she'd married, when he'd stolen a kiss from the shy debutant under the mistletoe at his mother's Winter Ball last year, but he'd managed to stop at just that one kiss. As a widow, she presented less risk to his single existence, she'd been married before so he no longer needed to ignore this startling attraction. He could be with her if she wanted him. She likely wouldn't see him as a potential husband so soon after losing her own.

However, given she was supposed to be alone, and her rather protective father far away tonight, he wouldn't retreat to another part of the building and leave her unprotected. He slid behind the door with a nod to Winifred.

"Who's there?" she asked, hurriedly straightening her attire. The adorable flush of color to her cheeks sent his pulse racing.

"It's Lord Justin, Mrs. Moore. Might I have a word?"

Tristan shook his head, warning her not to open the door to his brother. He could imagine the beetle-browed clunch, hat in hand, hopeful gleam in his eye. The fool wouldn't usurp Tristan's place in Winifred's presence.

"I'm sorry, Lord Justin. The book you were looking for hasn't been found yet, but we'll send word to the Hall the moment we make any discovery," Winifred replied without opening the door. She pressed a hand to the wood, and Tristan couldn't help but cover her fingers with his.

"Oh, all right then. But let me know the minute you find it. Goodnight, Mrs. Moore."

Justin's disappointed tone brought a smile to Tristan's lips.

"Goodnight, sir. Pleasant dreams."

Tristan choked. Justin wasn't likely to have any of those. Heavy footsteps faded while Winifred's skin turned a fiery red. He retrieved her glass from the table. "Your wine, sweetheart."

The endearment rolled off his tongue easily and shockingly loud. Winifred accepted the wine, and hastily took a sip. Disconcerted by his slip, Tristan turned his attention to uncovering the cheese and bread he'd stolen from the cavernous kitchen at Staplehurst Hall. Too little for a lovers' feast, but he hoped Winifred didn't mind.

He drew a chair and bade her sit before he pulled his close to hers. "It is good to see you home again."

Another healthy blush crept up her cheeks. "I did get the impression you were pleased to see me."

"Definitely pleased." He sliced some cheese and handed it to her. Their fingers brushed, and he wished the meal over so they could get to more pleasurable activities. But there were questions he simply had to have answered before the evening progressed. He'd been in London when he'd heard of her sudden marriage and at the time he'd been unsettled by the news. "How did Moore manage to compromise you so easily?"

Winifred glanced away. "My father fell ill, essentially confined to bed. He refused to let me run the shop alone, but I had to go out to fetch medicine from the apothecary. Moore walked me home a few times, despite the fact I asked him to desist. One day, he kissed me where someone could see. The town wouldn't hear of any other outcome. I had no choice. Father's health had not recovered enough for my comfort, so I consented to save him distress and assured him a marriage to Moore pleased me."

"And now?"

Winifred frowned. "I cannot be unhappy that Moore is gone. We were not a good match."

Tristan scrubbed a hand across his jaw. "I never imagined the union would be. Moore behaved poorly among men. Did he hurt you?"

"Not really, I suppose."

A fiery blush swept over her cheeks, and he wondered if her skin heated like that all over. He'd find out soon enough. But for now, he'd change the subject to something that might amuse. "Mother mentioned Miss Wheaton is becoming something of a trial but I never quite believed her until today."

When she snorted a laugh, then quickly covered her mouth, he guessed his mother had spoken only a portion of the truth. Winifred cleared her throat. "She does have a way with people."

"Clearly not a nice one. I'm told Miss Wheaton feels she could organize the local amusements to suit her taste."

Winifred's gaze snapped to his. "I imagine Her Grace would not have cared for that."

"Mother blistered the walls with her outraged silence."

Her laugh, a delicate sound that stirred his desire, echoed around the chamber. "I cannot believe she has left Miss Wheaton with her ego in place."

Tristan shrugged. "Mother has developed an absurd expectation that Miss Wheaton, and quite a few other local young ladies, might tempt me into marriage. Rather than risk alienating a potential daughter-in-law so early, I fear she's biding her time until her advice cannot be ignored."

As Winifred's face drained of color, he regretted his frank words. She would have been one of their numbers once, hoping to catch his eye like all the young ladies in the district. He had no desire for marriage—not at twenty-three —but a night spent between a willing widow's sheets interested him completely.

"The duchess is undoubtedly correct in her methods," she mumbled.

"Goodness, don't let my mother hear you say that. You'll become her favorite, and you know how that will go."

Winifred kept a straight face a moment before an impish grin spread. "I'm honestly not that fond of butterfly hunting."

Tristan leaned on the table. "Believe me; no one else she's dragged along is, either."

They finished their simple meal, light banter stretching the moments until they'd consumed everything, and then Winifred rinsed the dirty glasses. Tristan admired the way her dark gown clung to her curves, aware of a growing desire to stand and wrap her tight in his arms to continue their embraces. But he'd probably become carried away. She deserved better than a rough taking upon the kitchen table, and he wanted hours of leisure to explore and excite the good widow.

Eventually, she finished her fussing and faced him. Tristan stood, holding out a hand to draw her close again. Her work-reddened fingers were cold against his lips. "To bed with you."

He kissed her fingers again, leaned over to pick up the lit candle, and tugged her toward the staircase. As shadows danced over the walls, he wondered if she would change her mind about entertaining him. Yet Winifred hurried ahead, leading him up the narrow stairs toward a moonlit bedchamber without a single falter to her step.

The plain room held everything he desired —a bed large enough for the two of them. He kicked the door shut, then blew out the candle and set it aside.

Cool air swirled from the open window. Tristan pulled Winifred toward him, determined to keep her warm.

She shivered.

"Nervous?"

Winifred relaxed in his arms. "No, not at all. Strange, isn't it?"

"Delightful," he whispered. "Come here, let me love you."

When she sank against his chest, he gave into the urge to capture her lips. This time, he kissed with greater pressure, sliding his tongue along their seam until she gasped. He invaded her mouth, holding her waist tight between his hands. She was quick to respond, meeting him with her tongue. She tasted of cheese and sweet wine. Delicious. The sweetest bundle he'd ever handled.

The buttons at her back slipped undone easily under his practiced fingers. He released her lips and kissed across her cheek to her ear. He feathered his tongue across her lobe, hearing her shuddering intake of breath as she wriggled, then he kissed her neck.

The black gown and chemise slid from one shoulder, and he pressed a hard kiss to naked flesh as he tugged her widow's weeds downward to hang from her hips.

Moonlight illuminated full breasts, her nipples hardening to tight points in the cool air. With a moan, he dropped low to capture one in his mouth.

She stiffened. It seemed her husband had been a selfish man. Her upper body angled away from Tristan's lips, but he held her still, raining light kisses over her plump skin until she relaxed. Winifred may never have experienced pleasure in her marriage, but she would tonight. Tristan shaped her heavy breast with his fingers and took the peak deeply into his mouth. A moan rattled through her chest as she curled her fingers into his hair, hesitantly at first, then with more enthusiasm as he flicked her nipple with the tip of his tongue.

When he shifted to her other breast, she pressed her chest toward him.

After several moments of gasping encouragement, Tristan caught the back of her gown again and continued undoing buttons. The dark bombazine, along with the chemise, slid over her hips and down her legs. Black didn't suit her. He'd thought that the minute he'd laid eyes on her again. Tristan skimmed her body with his hands, dropping to his knees at her feet.

Above him, Winifred rubbed her fingers through his hair. When he pressed his lips to her softly rounded belly, she moaned deep in her throat. As tempting as the position might be, he wanted her in bed. He wanted to concentrate on her pleasure and not worry if she had the strength to remain standing.

He rose and swept her into his arms. Winifred yelped. Giving her a soft smile, he deposited her on the bed. She moved restlessly while he stripped his upper body, then sat next to her to remove his boots. When he'd struggled out of them, he turned. Win lay prone, knees together, her body tense again. Tristan smoothed a hand up her stocking clad leg and drew her knee outward a little so he could see the heart of her. He met her gaze. "Beautiful."

Her lips lifted into a timid smile. Her body relaxed.

Without removing his trousers, Tristan slowly lowered himself to the bed at her side and rested his hand flat on her belly. He would not pounce on her. She'd stiffened the moment he moved closer. When he captured her lips again, she fluttered her hands over his skin as if she didn't know where to place them.

"Touch me," he murmured.

Winifred's grip on his arms firmed. "Where?"

"Anywhere, everywhere, nowhere is off limits."

She curled one arm high about his shoulders, fingers threading through his hair until she found his ear. The soft, curious touch dragged a groan from his chest. He swept his hand up her body until he cupped her breast. When she didn't stiffen, he bent his head.

Again, he pleasured her breasts, licking them, lightly biting the firm peaks until her body undulated. He pressed more of his weight against her, pushing his erection firmly into the softness of her thigh.

Winifred's desperate moan echoed around

the chamber. She dug her fingers into the muscles of his shoulders. Tristan shifted his weight to one arm and slid his hand down her body, delving between her legs. Her breath rasped across his neck. Her gasp sent chills down his spine. He took her mouth, reveling in her sweet responsiveness as he parted her lower lips, invading where only her undeserving husband had gone before. She sobbed, and Tristan lifted his head. Confusion clouded her eyes.

"Shh, sweetheart. I'll make everything better soon," he promised.

Her thighs relaxed again, allowing him to explore. Gratifying dampness coated his fingertips. She appeared as keen for him as he was for her. He let his fingers slide over her soft skin, paused to circle her entrance, and then touched her nub. Winifred arched her hips off the bed, and he rode out her shock, pressing light kisses to her lips until she quieted.

"Almost an innocent," he whispered as he circled her clitoris with steady pressure.

After a few strokes, Winifred's labored breaths hinted her release hovered moments away. He couldn't wait another moment to join with her. He sat up, ripped open his trousers, and pushed them over his hips.

His stiff length ached for her, so he lay

down again, settled between her legs, and butted against her curls.

Winifred's eyes widened as he pushed her knees apart, positioned, and then joined with her. Her shriek hinted at surprised pleasure, a fact that kept him moving, despite her tight, clinging heat. He turned his head to kiss her, held her close as he kept a steady pace of thrusts and hip rolls.

As she dug her fingers into his flesh, Tristan urged her legs about his waist, settling deeper into her body with every thrust. She displayed no false modesty, but also gave no hint she realized how her damp heat delighted him. In all his years of wenching, he'd never known so warm a welcome.

As she clutched at his shoulders, he slipped a hand between their bodies to arouse her further. He slicked his fingers, feeling his cock enter and leave her body. On impulse, he replaced his cock with his fingers. Winifred opened her legs wider, taking him deeper, dampening his fingers up to his knuckles. He couldn't take any more. He returned to her and thrust his cock inside, hard, fast, with little finesse and even less control.

Winifred grasped his thigh, pulling him deeper into her heat. He fought the urge to spend, strumming her hard nub with quick flicks of his fingers. Winifred's moans were gratifying. He'd known she'd be passionate, but this was more than he'd anticipated. Just when he wondered whether she'd find fulfillment, she arched her back, and her scream rent the air around them, triggering his own release.

He shuddered inside her, and when he found his breath again, he realized he'd crushed her into an awkward position.

Tristan rolled to his back, gasping. "My apologies, too quick yet again."

Beside him, Winifred laughed. An earthy chuckle he hadn't expected, and one that sent tremors through him. "If that was quick, my lord, then you need to compare notes with other men. I fear you killed me."

He faced her, lying on his side so he could see her better. Her tousled hair spread across the pillow and over the side of the mattress. She studied him with her heavy-lidded gaze. Beautiful, exciting, and all his. Tristan kissed her again, flattening his palm over her quivering belly, tracing swirling patterns upon her skin. She shied away from the touch, but he didn't let her slip from the bed. He held her in place, one hand wedged between her legs to hold her still.

"I'm not finished with you yet." He grinned, hoping she didn't have any plans to sleep tonight.

Winifred arched a brow. "A man with stamina?"

"Damn right. You'll not leave this bed 'till morning."

CHAPTER THREE

EARLY MORNING SUNLIGHT woke Winifred from a deep sleep. She sat up and glanced around her bedroom nervously, half expecting someone to walk in and find her naked in bed. What had she done?

She'd spent the night entertaining an experienced rake, that's what.

Winifred pulled the sheet high up her chest, overwhelmingly conscious of her nakedness and the way her body ached from the past night's exertions. Ramsbury seemed to bring out a side of her she'd never believed existed, and she was more than a little embarrassed by her wanton behavior.

But she also felt enlightened.

Her husband had done nothing more than rut in her like a beast, with no desire to show her kindness or pleasure of any sort.

Like most respectable young ladies her age —correction, previously respectable—she'd gone to her marriage bed a virgin, ignorant, a state Peter had quickly robbed her of with no ceremony or care. He'd taken her bright future and ruined her present with his callous treatment on their wedding night. Afterward, she'd cried silently over the aching pain, determined not to reveal her discomfort. Or risk waking him. Moore had come to her bed every night, and every night he had treated her with the same, rough indifference. But what she'd hated most was the way his gaze followed her as she carried out her wifely duties in the hovel he'd taken her to, reminding her without words of what would follow when he blew out the candle.

If not for his death, she'd never have known how truly pleasurable intimate relations could be. Ramsbury was a talented man. And a thorough one. He'd made her beg for the end to come more than once. She blushed at the memory.

Warmth stroked her back. When she turned, she found Tristan looking at her, his bright blue eyes filled with mischief. Seeing him awake in her sunlit chamber, surrounded by her simple possessions, filled her with dread.

Would he look down on her when he noticed how shabby her few furnishings were?

The way he held her gaze, unblinking and direct, made her hope he might not notice at all. Winifred set her chin to her shoulder. "Good morning."

His lips curled up in a way she'd come to appreciate. His expression reminded her of kisses and the drugging pleasure he brought. "That, it definitely is, but a late one by the look of it. You exhausted me, woman."

She couldn't help but smile that a man of his reputation claimed she exhausted him. Never before had she gone a night with so little sleep, nor had she ever experienced half the intimacies they'd shared. She let her gaze travel the exposed length of him, noting his aroused state. "You look no worse for wear, despite all your complaints."

He flexed his hips. "Compliments. Not complaints. Come here, Win."

"Yes, my lord."

As he curled his hand around her skull, Winifred fell into to his embrace. The heat of his skin scalded as she wrapped her fingers around his broad shoulders, feeling the hard strength usually hidden beneath clothes. She'd been cozy and warm all night without the benefit of a fire because the viscount had never allowed her to stray from his side for more than a few moments.

He pulled her atop him, spread her legs so they fell to the mattress on either side of his thighs, and nudged at her core with his cock.

"Call me by my name." His breath whispered across her cheek and then he kissed her there too.

She shuddered. "Tristan, you need to be on your way. And I need to open my father's shop."

"All I need this morning is you, Win." He pressed his hard length inside with agonizing slowness. An inch that made her desperate for the rest of him. "I want to know you'll remember me through the long day ahead. I want to know that lurking beneath those polite smiles you give away to your customers is a well-satisfied woman. Ride me."

After the wicked pleasures of the previous night, she had a fair idea what he meant. He wanted her on top, rising from the mattress, so he could see what the darkness had withheld. Although her belly quaked to be so exposed and bold, she set her hands to his muscled chest and rose, sliding her knees beneath her so she sat astride his hips. His cock slipped inside an inch more—an inch that wrenched a groan from her chest. When Tristan's slow perusal over parts of her body best left hidden from the light of day ended where they joined, Winifred couldn't hold back her blush. He would see. *Everything.* Would he be displeased? She hadn't thought she could be shocked further, but his bright eyes widened, and he tilted his head so he could glimpse more. Her skin grew fiery hot.

He looked up and held her gaze. "You've kept your beauty well hidden, Win. I've never touched a more breathtaking woman."

"You're too kind," Winifred murmured, then chuckled at the absurdity of her response. She could have uttered those words in the duchess's drawing room and not have been looked at twice. She was naked, for heaven's sake, and half-impaled on the wicked Lord Ramsbury.

The viscount smiled too.

Suddenly, half-impaled was nowhere near enough. But she forced herself to slow down, to admire her lover as he deserved. He truly was magnificent to behold. She slid her fingers over his tight abdomen, smoothed the sparse hair on his muscled chest, watching his skin ripple with obvious strength.

She sank low and impaled herself fully, stopping only when she had him buried deep in her needy body.

Winifred reveled in the gasp she wrenched from Tristan's throat, in the way his hips arched from the mattress in pleasure, pushing deeper into her. She was in control of their tryst now. She could deny him by not moving. Deprive him of the friction they both craved. The temptation held her still, though she wanted nothing more than to move, to hear the viscount's deep rumble of satisfaction again.

"I believe Mrs. Moore has found a way to bring me to heel." He curled his hands around her hips and tightened his grip. "But the lady has forgotten that it is never wise to deny her lord." He lifted her along his shaft, then lowered her again, proving he remained firmly in control of their affair. His strength let him have his way no matter what. But then he let her go and tucked his arms behind his head.

Deprived of his delicious touch, she didn't know what to do.

He must have sensed her confusion because he suddenly grinned. "I am yours to rule, my dear lady. Do what you wish with me."

The possibilities were endless, but she needed to move. Winifred rose to the point where he might slip from her body, then descended just as slowly. Tristan groaned, so she did it again—at the same, painfully slow pace, feeling desire build until her toes tingled.

Could she appear more scandalous?

Tristan seemed happy with his position. His wicked, blue eyes glowed so brightly she stilled, mesmerized by his handsome face. Tristan curled his fingers around her hips once more, and with his strength supporting her weight and guiding her pleasure, she maintained the steady pace, but her inner thighs quaked.

Tristan released her and her strength faltered, but he thrust up, working into her body with slow deliberation while he delved between her legs with firm pressure. Winifred could die in truth this time from the pleasure of those fingers.

She could smell her own arousal, heard the wet slide of his cock as he entered and left her body. He spread her lower lips with his fingers, slicked them, then dragged them across her aching bud. Winifred's breath rattled from her chest. She took a deep, steadying breath, and reached behind her to touch his stones. She tugged a little on the skin. Tristan groaned as she rolled the tight sac between her fingers.

"Wicked woman," Tristan grunted. "I should never have taught you that."

Pleased she'd managed to surprise him, she fingered one of his balls, capturing him with the gentle touch he preferred. Tristan gasped and thrust faster, lifting her higher into the air with each movement.

A fierce ache built, centering where they joined. Fearing her end drew near, Winifred closed her eyes. She did not want her last glimpse of earthly life to be the viscount's laughing eyes. For some unfathomable reason, he seemed absurdly amused when the pleasure overtook her. Maybe that was the reason for his splendid reputation. He made women feel special.

Her desire peaked, sharp, hot, and irresistible. She cried out as Tristan rammed high into her body, lifting her knees from the bed, his groans blending with hers.

Winifred fell to his chest, gasping for breath and sanity. How could he believe she would forget him during the long day ahead? The night and morning were etched into her body and her mind for eternity.

Tristan's sweaty flesh singed her cheek. She shifted, eased his length from her body, and slumped to the cool sheets. She'd have a hard time thinking of this morning without a telling blush scalding her skin. How on earth would she be able to look at him in public?

She'd need to come up with some plan to control her unfortunate blushing. Such a reaction in the presence of a gentleman Devizes's society believed she barely knew would cause endless speculation about her behavior. She could not have that. She had to make sure there were no repercussions that could affect her father's position in town. Poor Father—his consequence had suffered quite enough because of her past mistakes.

Tristan rolled from the bed. "I have to go."

Gingerly, Winifred sat and reached for her chemise, watching the play of muscles along his back and thighs as he snatched up his clothing from the floor. She wished she could touch him again. But their time was over. He had to leave, to return to his privileged life, and she had her father's struggling bookshop to run.

Her legs were a little shaky as she stood to slip on a robe and tie it tight around her waist. But before she'd finished fussing with the knot, Tristan snaked an arm around her hips. He held her hard against him, and she realized the man had a gift for speedy dressing. He simply needed his coat and greatcoat from downstairs to look presentable.

"Thank you for a pleasant evening. You were so breathtaking I can scarcely drag myself away. May I call on you again?"

She turned in the circle of his arms as a smile burst free. "That would be lovely."

Tristan kissed the tip of her nose. It tickled, and she squirmed. "More than lovely. But where can we meet? Does your father go away often?"

Winifred's smile froze. She was the viscount's lover now. But she hadn't fallen so low she'd consider becoming his country mistress. "My father rarely leaves the shop for long."

"Ah, well, we'll arrange something."

Winifred clenched her hands together over her trembling stomach. Did he plan to visit her when he had the time, then return to his normal life? Well, she had a life too. And she had to be able to hold her head up in society, or the scandal of disgrace would force her to leave the district. She had to be certain he understood last night and this morning was an aberration. One not to be repeated.

She desperately tried to find the best way to deter him from suggesting she be his mistress out loud. She couldn't bear the humiliation of hearing those words, so she decided to deliberately misunderstand him. "Wonderful. My father enjoys your visits, you know. He appreciates discussing his latest inventory with an intelligent mind."

Tristan's jaw dropped a little, and she realized he did expect her to jump at the chance for a more permanent arrangement. She stepped out of his arms.

The viscount followed, but didn't touch. "I am always eager for intelligent conversation."

"My father will be more than happy to have you call on him during business hours." She lifted her gaze to find him frowning. "Hmm... Well, perhaps you'd best be on your way. I have quite a bit to do today. Please use the back door as you leave."

Tristan remained still a long moment. After she offered no more encouragement to discuss further meetings, he bowed. She dropped a formal curtsey, and he left the chamber. Winifred followed him downstairs. Denying herself the viscount's touch was the right thing to do, no matter how much she wished she hadn't. He slipped into his coat, then greatcoat, with neat, precise movements.

At the rear door, he turned back. "Have I said something to offend, Win?"

"Hardly that, my lord. But I do have my reputation to consider. My father and I must live here without any hint of further scandal, so I beg you to be discreet on your journey home."

Tristan pursed his lips as if in thought. "Get me a book."

"My lord?"

"A book might account for my early morning visit. If asked, you can claim I roused you far too early from your bed because I wished to please my mother. You will be believed. Today is her birthday."

Winifred doubted such a deception would work, but headed for the books without argument, trying to decide what Her Grace's taste might be. The duchess rarely patronized her father's shop. After all, Staplehurst Hall library held thousands of books. "Forgive me if this is inappropriate. This is a recent addition to the library—a gothic novel. The duchess might find the tale amusing."

She held the book out to him, her hand trembling with nervousness. How strange. She'd bared her body to his gaze and his thorough touch all through the long hours of the night, but dealing with him in broad daylight, half-dressed among the musty tomes of the lending library, unsettled her to an alarming degree. He took the book but also captured her hand and pressed a lingering kiss to her sensitive skin.

She couldn't possibly be aroused so easily, or again. Yet that brief touch of warm lips and breath forced a pant from her.

Lord Ramsbury tucked the book under his arm, fished out some coins—exactly enough to cover the book's expense—and laid them on the counter before walking to the front door. Winifred hurried after him, panicked that he intended to be so brazen.

"Thank you for the book. I'm sure my mother will enjoy it. If anyone asks, you can say all manner of rude things about me waking you to buy the duchess a present."

She clutched her robe tight about her neck. "I couldn't do that."

Tristan frowned. "You will to preserve your reputation. I want no harm to come to you because of last night. Lock the door after me, will you?"

"Of course, my lord, I'm barely dressed."

Those bright blue eyes skimmed over her thin robe, and a flush of heat swept over her cheeks once more. "Please don't remind me. I'm having enough trouble convincing myself to leave at this moment. You look beautiful, all tousled from our tryst."

Winifred blushed to the roots of her hair but managed to push him to the door. "Good-bye, my lord. I hope the duchess has an enjoyable birthday."

He tipped his hat and walked out. Winifred rushed to the door, bolted it again, then collapsed against the wood. Even after a night of the viscount's energetic loving, she wanted him back in her bed and buried between her legs.

She shook herself. It was over. An opportunity for dalliance might never come her way again. But oh, how she would hold the memories tightly to her chest when she slept alone at night. Feeling renewed, she rushed for the stairs and the busy day ahead.

CHAPTER FOUR

THE CHURCHYARD GATE yielded to Tristan's light touch as he stepped through, impatience riding him hard. The days since he'd shared Win's bed had dragged unbearably. Behind the gate, the voices of Devizes's good and honorable society rose in polite discussion. So far, no one had noticed him slip away from the church steps, because his intentions this morning were definitely not good and certainly not entirely honorable. He had a vital mission to undertake, and although neither the present circumstances nor the location were the best, he would make the most of the opportunity.

Mrs. Winifred Moore knelt several yards away, bent over some family gravestones and unaware of his presence. She laid a simple string of wildflowers over the grass-covered mound and arranged them into a heart shape. Tristan moved closer to read the inscription.

Felicity Ann Davey, 1798 to 1811, Beloved Daughter.

And Win's younger sister.

Unwilling to disturb her quiet contemplation, he waited patiently until she'd finished her fussing. The minute she sat back, he spoke. "I remember she had a laugh that would set all the other young girls to giggling."

Win turned, but she didn't smile. Her eyes were tear-filled. He slipped a hand under her elbow to help her stand. "Felicity loved her practical jokes."

Awareness of Win's scent, the heady breath of peppermint that lingered about her, slammed into him. He worked hard to control his physical reaction. "A practice you often scolded her for, I suspect."

"If I'd known—" Win shook her head. "She simply would not behave properly around certain people, as she should have done. You, in particular, if memory serves."

Tristan smiled and decided to confess to something he'd always believed hilariously funny. "Do you remember the day when Felicity wanted to return home through the little-used woodland path close to the dower house, and you were determined to take the proper track? I happened to come upon your disagreement. And though you never noticed me, Felicity did. Once you had stormed off for home, she convinced me to escort her through the woods. She assured me she would refuse to marry me should we be discovered together. I couldn't let her wander the woods alone. So, I extracted her promise not to become my wife under any circumstances, then held out my arm. I like to believe her later smiles were because of that day. We were co-conspirators against society, you see."

Instead of laughing with him, Win dropped her chin to her chest. "I feared she'd run all the way home. I scolded her for a week for behaving like a hoyden."

"The truth was far worse. She was more devious than you realized." Tristan had liked little Felicity, despite the large gap in their ages. He'd never met another young woman, just a girl, really, with such a visible joy of life. Perhaps she had known, somehow, a brief existence was all she would get. "A minx if ever there was one."

Win laughed, but the shake of her body alerted him his fingers were skimming over her black glove quite improperly for the setting. He let his hand fall away. "Were you to visit with your mother as well?"

"Yes, but I've laid flowers already."

Tristan peered around her to the next headstone. A small posy lay at the top of the grave. Adelade Davey, Win's mother, had been an astoundingly elegant woman, despite her low position in Devizes's society. He'd admired her at eighteen years of age, the year he took a more serious interest in the opposite sex and found much to tempt him.

Not that he'd considered Win's mother as a potential bed partner, but she became the standard to which he held most women. Her easy grace, uncommon courtesy, and awareness of her social position endeared her to him. Mrs. Davey had never pushed herself or her daughters forward and was well liked by the townsfolk.

Many had mourned Mrs. Davey's sudden death, Tristan's mother included. Her Grace had even sent the reduced family to one of the duke's lesser properties, where they might recover from the dreadful loss in privacy.

Win's looks were a great deal like her mother's. She had that same quiet dignity, even in the throes of passion and directly after. The passion Win hid so well from those around her had kept Tristan's thoughts firmly fixed on her and on how to get her alone again. She was more reclusive than a monk.

"I trust all is well at the bookshop." He glanced around, surreptitiously. "And that your father had no cause for questions. I fear I foolishly left the half-drunk bottle of wine behind."

"Yes. I mean, no." Her cheeks pinked with color. "His return was uneventful."

"That is excellent news." He adjusted his sleeve, grasping for the correct phrase to make his intentions clear without being vulgarly blunt. He wasn't sure she understood exactly what he'd meant to offer the first time. "I wondered if I might be the recipient of a further invitation soon. We seem well suited in passion."

Win's eyes widened. "As I believe I mentioned previously, the lending library is open from ten 'til four, Monday to Friday. You are welcome to visit within those hours."

"That wasn't what I meant. I wanted to offer you—"

Winifred's sudden hand gesture silenced him. "Don't you dare make that offer. I'm not interested."

Tristan gulped at the hard edge to her words. Damn it, that wasn't the least bit encouraging. Perhaps he needed to woo her a bit before she let him share her bed again.

Instead of engaging in a public debate, during which anyone might overhear them, Tristan offered his arm. "Mrs. Moore, perhaps you might permit me to escort you home."

Win licked her lips. "That is kind of you, my lord, but altogether inappropriate."

Tristan adopted a bored mien. "Mrs. Moore, a gentleman may escort a widow about the town, in broad daylight, without the slightest hint of scandal attaching to her name. I promise you, I shall behave and offer nothing but the highest of courtesy for the duration of our travels together. No one will gossip."

She glanced about, clearly thinking it over. "I suppose you could be correct."

"Of course I'm correct." He checked over his shoulder and spied his mother bearing down. "We shall speak to the duchess first? I doubt she will raise an imperious eyebrow at my intentions. If my memory serves, she is quite fond of you."

Before Win could reply, the Duchess of Devizes demanded their attention. "My boy, so this is where you got to. Ah, Mrs. Moore."

"Your Grace," Win murmured.

Tristan offered a brief smile as Win bobbed

the necessary curtsey. "Just paying my respects, Mother."

The duchess glanced beyond them. "Poor Adelade. I still expect to see her in town. Occasionally, your father will speak, Mrs. Moore, as if they had recently parted company."

"I know," Win whispered, a delicious, pink blush brightening her cheeks. She stared down at her fingers. "He cannot seem to help himself."

The duchess squeezed Win's hand, an extremely odd and personal gesture for her to make in public. "They were very much in love."

Again, Win's smile held a touch of sadness. Tristan wished to every saint that he could see her real smile again. The one she used when in his arms. Determined to distract her, Tristan tucked Win's arm into his.

"Do excuse us, Mother," he said. "Since the day has turned out so fair, I thought Mrs. Moore might enjoy a quiet walk home to boost her spirits. She seems a bit cast down after Mr. Mitchell's sermon."

The duchess's lips twitched. "All that fire and brimstone is enough to unsettle the hardiest of souls, let alone a widow. Do be on your way, my dears. I shall inform Mr. Davey that his daughter is in good hands." The duchess laid her hand over Win's, where it curled lightly about Tristan's arm, and squeezed. "It is good to see you about again, child."

With that, the duchess swept back the way she had come, collected her husband, and steered him toward where Tristan hoped Mr. Davey stood. He would not like Mr. Davey to worry for his daughter, and the duchess would set his mind to rights.

"You see," Tristan murmured as he led Win through another gateway and onto the narrow path away from the babbling congregation. "I have the duchess's approval for the walk. None shall dare to gainsay her."

She didn't reply, but followed his lead without any hint of hesitation. Sunlight gleamed over her silky, soft, auburn hair, sending a bolt of lust straight to his groin. He wanted to touch her as intimately as he had their night together, but the setting, a country walk, and a short one at that, hardly seemed a fitting location.

He would have to be content with her chaste company.

"What new books did your father acquire on his trip?"

Win raised her gaze to his and detailed the lending library's newest editions. Her soft, melodious voice washed over him and kept him rapt with such startling attention they reached her home in what felt like no time at all.

At the door, he took off his hat while Win turned the key in the lock. He made no move to follow. She was a widow, it was true, but a skittish one, and one determined to appear respectable at all times. And he'd promised to behave, much as he might regret the loss of this opportunity. "Mrs. Moore, thank you for your delightful company. I wish you a pleasant day."

She appeared startled at his quick farewell, but hastily dropped an elegant curtsey to his bow. He then turned for the street. If he were a betting man, he'd say she'd expected him to pester her. He wasn't that big a cad. If she wanted nothing further from him, then he wouldn't stay where he wasn't wanted.

Once on the dusty street, he tipped his hat and strode for the church where his younger brother, Justin, held his waiting mount.

"I see the widow Moore gave you your marching orders," his brother quipped. "I told you I had a better chance."

Tristan longed to blurt out the truth of his conquest over the widow Moore, as he had often proclaimed his previous encounters with willing women. But something held him back. He refused to let Justin relegate Win to that class of conquered females. Her passion was quite superior, in all respects. He took the reins, ready for the boredom of another day, or more, without the widow in his arms. Despite his willingness, mere moments ago, not to harass Win, he considered giving the woman one more opportunity to change her mind. His reversal dragged a laugh from his chest.

His brother scowled. "And what's so damned funny?"

Tristan glanced at his brother. Lean, rail-thin, and convinced of his universal appeal, Justin acted as if he could have everything he wanted, except for the title. Justin had never coveted being first born.

"Nothing that concerns you." He stroked his horse's nose, knowing Justin would take the bait and continue their disagreement. He could use a spot of amusement since Winifred Moore's siren call plagued him daily. He needed a plan to convince her to return to his bed. "I still believe you have no chance at all with Mrs. Moore, Justin. Why not admit defeat?"

Justin's horse danced, proving Tristan had

managed to unsettle both his brother and his brother's mount. "You can boast of your prowess endlessly, Ramsbury, but someone must win the lady. I aim to do that. I'll even wager that I have her garter before the week is out."

Tristan forced his hands to relax on the reins. He didn't like the idea of Justin anywhere near his woman. "A week? Really, Justin, you have all the finesse of a leave-taking sailor after six months at sea."

"Fast or slow, I get the job done," he grumbled.

"But are the ladies thoroughly satisfied?" Tristan snorted, deliberately goading his cocky brother. "You'd know for certain, if you weren't dashing off after the next set of stockings so quickly."

His brother's face flushed a deep red, an unattractive color that hinted Justin struggled to control his temper. But he calmed himself with the slow, deliberate breathing their fencing instructor had recommended. "I will not stay here and be insulted about my ability to satisfy a woman. When we return to London, we shall see whose luck is better. I say we pick a woman and see who can entice her to share her bed first."

Tristan swung up into the saddle. "I'm not returning to Town as yet. I'll be staying here for the summer."

"Good God, why?"

Tristan tightened the reins to reassure his restless mount while he considered how to answer. "Father has been pressuring me for years to take a greater interest in the estate. He's not getting any younger, you know. I have a lot to learn."

Justin snorted. "If you're not careful, the ladies in the district, widow and debutant alike, will attempt to entrap you into marriage. They'll have you turned about before you can blink. Are you prepared for that kind of campaign?"

"I know how to deal with the ladies."

Because unlike you, Justin, I'm not afraid of a challenge. And Winifred Moore challenged him like no other.

CHAPTER FIVE

THE LETTER, when it arrived three days later, completely shocked Winifred. She stared at the elegant paper and even more elegant lettering containing her directions, and the thick seal on the back, with intense dread. Such a distinguished-looking letter did not belong in her shabby kitchen. But, given the Duchess of Devizes had sent Winifred a personal missive, it couldn't be ignored.

Heavens, what had she done?

Winifred broke the seal to read the neat script, trying to keep the tremors from her hand. The duchess had invited her to take tea that afternoon at three o'clock. The shock of it all kept her immobile.

Refusal was impossible.

Attendance—her worst nightmare.

She couldn't take tea with her lover's mother.

"What have you there, Mrs. Moore?" Her father hovered at her side, his gaze fixed upon the obviously expensive missive clutched in her hands.

Winifred swallowed the sob she wanted to utter. He wouldn't understand her terror or the inadvisability of attending. He would expect her to be happy over the invitation. It was a mark of distinction to be included in the duchess's circle. She did her best to summon up a portion of the required level of enthusiasm. "The duchess has invited me for tea this afternoon."

Her father's eyes gleamed as he glanced about him, his shoulders rising from their habitual stoop. His reaction made her realize it was the first time since her mother's death he appeared like the aristocrat in exile he was. Winifred hadn't imagined the extent losing her mother had taken on his sense of self-worth until now. So she forced a brighter smile, determined not to see his pride fall again.

"Do you know what this means, Daughter?"

"Her Grace is bored?" Winifred asked playfully. The whole town gossiped about the duchess's habit of inviting eligible young ladies of the district into her circle. But the novelty soon wore off, the chit eventually married below the duchess's notice, and she never invited them to tea again. The older ladies claimed Her Grace had a thing for matchmaking, yet Winifred couldn't see the benefit.

Marriage hadn't been a pleasant experience.

"This means Her Grace has forgiven you for your unfortunate marriage and wishes you all possible happiness." He dragged the letter from her numb fingers, read the instructions, then held it tightly to his chest. "We are saved."

Winifred tried to be happy. After all, her marriage had caused him no small amount of stress and discomfort. Being compromised by a gentleman of such low standing as Mr. Moore tended to reflect badly on the father of the bride. For a time, her father had suffered the snubs alone. But when she'd returned home, widowed, and apparently contrite enough to appease the town's morals, he'd become one of their number again.

It helped that Winifred was rarely seen, rarely the center of attention, and perfectly happy with that arrangement. Or at least she had been until Lord Ramsbury had shared her bed.

She turned away. The past few days she'd been restless. Did she want to take tea with her lover's mother? Heavens, what if the duchess had noticed her son's early morning return and surmised what he'd been doing? Men never came in for censure after a night of wenching, but the woman... She shuddered. If the duchess had learned of that night, Winifred faced ruin beyond any hope of redemption.

Her father clutched at her arm, then tugged her to her feet. "Wear your best dress."

Gently, she disentangled herself from his excited grip. "I'll wear mourning, as I should, Papa. The town gossips would go up in flames otherwise. It's not even been three months."

Her father frowned at his feet but nodded. Despite the rare invitation, Winifred couldn't flout the rules of society without someone noticing or commenting on her behavior. She wouldn't make a spectacle of herself ever again.

Preparing for an audience with Her Grace wasn't so difficult, but the long walk to Staplehurst Hall tired her. Her black, bombazine gown absorbed every bit of the day's heat; her feet grew as heavy as lead, and by the time the grand entrance door appeared before her eyes, her nerves were frayed beyond repair.

Unfortunately, the first trial of the day came before Winifred even had a chance to knock.

"If you're looking for me, then you only have to turn around. Here I am, your willing and eager servant."

Winifred didn't turn at first. She knocked, to be certain she might have the limited protection of a servant as witness. Then, she executed a slow pivot. Lord Justin stood one step behind, too close for her comfort, too close to have any honorable intentions. His smile hinted he'd like nothing better than to devour her whole, a look he'd cast her way with tedious frequency. She wished he'd go away.

Winifred crowded the entrance, but fell in as the door opened behind her. Quick as lightning, a strong hand caught her fall and righted her without fuss.

"May I help you?" a voice asked.

She focused her gaze on the butler and away from the gentleman chuckling over her discomfort. "Yes. Her Grace sent me an invitation for tea. Could you inform her that Mrs. Moore has arrived?"

The butler cast a quick glance behind her,

scowling when he noticed Lord Justin hovering. He seemed to recognize her situation and appeared more than happy to aid her rescue. He led her into the blessedly cool interior, but Lord Justin followed and lounged against a wall, watching her intently. "My name is Brinkley, madam. I believe the duchess is expecting you directly. May I take your things?"

Winifred let out a breath, grateful not to be left alone in Lord Justin's company. She slipped off her best bonnet, casting a surreptitious glance at the nearest mirror. Her cheeks were frightfully bright, but she couldn't help it.

"The mirror doesn't do you justice," Lord Justin assured her.

Instead of answering, Winifred shot an angry glare at Tristan's brother. The one lapse in her education was the means and extent to which a widow might go to repulse an unwanted gentleman's advances. Prior to her marriage, she'd never been left alone much. But widows required no escorts, and she now appeared to be fair game to all classes of men. Lord Justin might require considerable discouragement.

"This way, Mrs. Moore."

Relieved, she followed the butler, flexing her fingers repeatedly in the hope of cooling her gloved hands before she reached the formal drawing room. She'd visited Staplehurst Hall before, for the Winter Ball, and knew she had little time to compose herself before facing the duchess.

Instead of leading Winifred to the formal drawing room on the left, as she expected, Brinkley led her past the staircase to a part of the Hall in which she'd never set foot. Opulent doors stood open, and the sound of animated chatter reached her ears.

As the butler announced her, three pairs of eyes pinned her in place. Winifred barely noticed Brinkley's departure. She was prey caught in a predator's sight.

Winifred hadn't realized the duchess's two sisters, the Ladies Herriot and Armitage, were in residence at Staplehurst Hall. They, along with the duchess, had reputations as the highest sticklers of the *ton*. Falling into their disfavor could ruin a girl's chances of making a good match. Debutants of rich, well-connected families were known to go to incredible lengths to gain even a nod from one of them. Getting through the afternoon unscathed would be a miracle.

Her shoulders sagged in defeat.

"My dear Mrs. Moore, do come sit down. You look quite exhausted."

The kind words were such a surprise, Winifred feared her mouth had fallen open. She pressed her lips together, moved forward as gracefully as she could despite the overwhelming urge to run away, and sank into the nearest armchair.

The rotund Lady Herriot passed a fan to Winifred. "Wave it about, girl, before you suffer a collapse. Never realized the day had turned so warm."

"Dezzie, call for some refreshments," Lady Armitage advised. "Something cool."

The Duchess of Devizes, or Dezzie, as her elder sister apparently called her, rushed to pull the bell, then swept back to her sister's side. "Perhaps we should have sent the carriage."

Winifred tried to get her breath back while the sisters bickered over her weary state without asking her opinion. Much was proposed then quickly dismissed, until she feared, and hoped, they had quite forgotten her.

"Ah, good, our refreshments," the duchess exclaimed with more enthusiasm than Winifred imagined possible.

Her sisters cooed. They fussed over the tray

with great delight, pronounced Cook an angel, then complimented Her Grace extensively for finding the perfect woman to spoil her and them all. Compliments passed frequently between the trio, but Winifred believed them sincere. The sisters were known to be slightly eccentric and extremely close. Yet they were not behaving quite the way she had expected. Other ladies had commented upon the lengthy silences, the refinement, and the lack of food. Today appeared a veritable feast.

"Tea with milk and sugar?" Lady Armitage asked.

"Black tea, thank you, my lady."

The sisters exchanged what could only be described as delighted expressions. The duchess's gaze pinned her in place. "Shrewsbury Cake or Princes Loaf."

"Oh, a Princes Loaf, please. I adore them."

The duchess appeared crestfallen at the news. Winifred ate the sticky, oozing confection with three pairs of eyes watching her swallow every mouthful. She hadn't had a Princes Loaf since the Winter Ball, but such extravagant dishes were frequently served at the duchess's table. Winifred couldn't determine why her eating preferences were so interesting to Her Grace, but she made sure to eat delicately until they returned to their conversation about the family's goings-on.

"And what do you think of my sons, Mrs. Moore?" The duchess asked suddenly. "Will they marry soon enough to please their mother?"

Luckily, Winifred was hot enough that her pink skin would still hide her discomfort. "I, ah, couldn't say, Your Grace."

The duchess's shrewd gaze skimmed over her appearance. Too thoughtfully for Winifred's comfort. "Hmm, I thought, perhaps, they might have indicated some preference recently. They have both been rather attentive to you of late."

No amount of exhaustion could hide Winifred's blush. She rapidly deployed the borrowed fan to cool her skin, but her heart sank as the duchess exchanged pointed looks with her sisters, a small smile playing around her mouth. It was foolish to imagine Her Grace had found her out, yet hadn't flown into a rage over her liaison with Tristan. But that smile hinted at a private vindication. She couldn't know for certain—she simply couldn't.

Win swallowed. "Yes, both of your sons have visited my father's shop of late and have expressed interest in particular books. I'm told

Lord Justin is searching for a misplaced personal journal, but we haven't found it yet within the shop."

The duchess smoothed her skirts. "And I believe I must thank you for choosing such a lovely book for Tristan to give me for my birthday, Mrs. Moore. My sisters and I are in raptures over the wicked count in it."

Winifred smiled, hoping the worst might be over. And it was for the rest of the tea, until it was time for her to depart.

"Dezzie dear, do ring for Ramsbury," Lady Herriot murmured, but her eyes were fixed on the last piece of Shrewsbury Cake. "Mrs. Moore still appears too flushed. I should hate to see her exhausted again so soon. I insist he escort her home."

Was that amusement twinkling in the woman's eyes? She hoped not.

Dear Dezzie nodded sagely, while Winifred's color surely rose to a bright pink again. Winifred plied her borrowed fan as Her Grace summoned her son and sat to wait his arrival, tapping her fingers on the arm of the chair.

Ramsbury strolled into the room. "You sent for me, Your Grace?"

Winifred's breath seized in her chest, withheld by shock, when their gazes connected. He was every bit as handsome today, fully dressed for riding, as he'd been the morning after their tryst, or in the churchyard days ago. To her alarm, she sensed a tightening of her breasts, her nipples forming hard points beneath the black bombazine. She also realized, if not for their esteemed company, she might well throw herself at Tristan to soothe the instant ache his presence evoked. She pressed her knees together to fight the hot desire.

"Mrs. Moore is greatly fatigued by the heat of the day," the duchess informed him. "Do be a dear boy and escort her home."

As Tristan rubbed at the light stubble on his jaw, Winifred forced air into her starved lungs. She hadn't seen him since the morning he'd walked her home from church. She had deliberately kept herself busy and hidden inside the shop all week. Given her refusal to continue their affair, would he be willing? "Your timing is perfect, as always. I'm heading to the village directly."

His expression was one of polite boredom, so much so she feared the request too much of an imposition. Winifred had refused his hints to extend their affair twice. Would he make his disappointment known to those around him?

The viscount turned a warm smile her way. "Mrs. Moore, if you are ready, I can take you with me now."

"Of course." Winifred gained her feet, but her body desperately wanted to close the space between them. However, she had to make the perfect goodbye. "Thank you for a lovely afternoon, Your Grace, Lady Herriot, Lady Armitage."

"Of course, my dear." The duchess smiled. "We shall look forward to seeing you on Friday at the same time."

Winifred gulped. "Visit again. Why, um, thank you for the invitation, Your Grace." Another tea? She'd never stand the strain.

"But of course." The duchess smiled at her sisters and received nods in return. "We have enjoyed our time together very much."

Out of the corner of her eye, Winifred noticed Tristan's mouth fall open. He shut it quickly, casting a puzzled glance at his mother before he held out his arm for Winifred. They calmly strolled from the room, yet the tension sizzling through her body was anything but serene. She fumbled with her hat, her breath churning fast while Tristan waited with apparent patience. She hoped the hovering butler didn't notice her discomfort, or gossip would spread like fire.

Tristan helped her into the waiting gig, firmly sliding his hands over her waist, and then filled the remaining space beside her. She tried to ignore the warmth of his thigh pressed tight against hers. She even managed to not show any physical reaction, but she was startlingly aware that a strong, desirable male touched her.

Tristan flicked the reins, setting the horse off at a sprightly pace for town, without a word. A bit of grit flicked up into her eye, and she ducked her head to try to remove it.

"Were they horrid to you?" Tristan asked, pressing his shoulder against hers.

"No. No, of course not. I have something in my eye."

And the dashed piece of grit wouldn't budge. She stripped off her gloves but it was no use. Her eye watered terribly.

"Hold on," he urged, as the gig rumbled over a bridge. He sent the horse into a tight turn immediately after, then onto a lane that did not lead to her home. Winifred clung to the rail and tried to see where he'd taken them, but her vision wasn't good. A house loomed before them —perhaps the dower house—from what little she could make out.

He drove the horse and gig into the empty stable then jumped down to tie them securely. He gripped her thighs and tugged Winifred toward the end of the bench. "Come here, and let me look at you."

Reluctantly, she accepted his help to disembark. She stood still while he took her face between his hands to stare into her watering eye. With slow, gentle care, he found and removed the offending bit of grit, and she blinked rapidly, pleased her eye no longer hurt.

"Thank you."

The devious grin should have warned her. "You are very welcome, indeed." Slowly, with obvious hesitation, Tristan pressed a slow, devastating kiss to her lips. Winifred sobbed and opened her mouth, impatiently flicking her tongue across his. He drew her tongue deeper into his mouth until she writhed against him for more. His kiss turned urgent, demanding, and she arched with pleasure. She had missed him this past week. More than she'd wanted to.

But she'd made it through the interview with his aunts without revealing a relationship with the duchess's son. To run the risk of discovery now seemed foolish. Winifred set her hands to his chest and pushed. "We shouldn't do this here."

CHAPTER SIX

DRAWING BACK, when Tristan wanted more, proved an immense struggle. But he had some control where Win was concerned. Little enough to remain a gentleman. Her dark eyes regarded him anxiously, so he relaxed his grip. "True. I have the perfect place in mind. Come this way."

He caught her hand to lead her from the stables, but she dug her heels in when faced with the empty dower house.

"That wasn't what I meant at all," she gasped and glanced around as though afraid someone would see them together. He honestly didn't care if someone did at that moment.

"You want privacy, yes?" He tilted his head, hoping she wouldn't protest that their desire wasn't mutual.

Her eyes gleamed with fierce hunger.

"None of the family comes here but me of late."

Still, she resisted. "Why just you? Do you bring all your lovers here?"

Her question, sharp and dripping with jealous tones, made him laugh. "Because I plan to move here soon. The duke and duchess are becoming too nosy about my affairs to make further co-habitation desirable." He set his hand to her cheek, peering deeply into her fathomless eyes to prove his next words true. "You were my last lover. I've not brought anyone here before."

She melted into him, so he took the opportunity to kiss her again before she changed her mind. The few days since he'd last done so faded as anticipation swiftly built. Win's sweet, responsive kisses were addictive. When he could lift his head away from her luscious lips, he hurried her toward the house.

The key stuck, as always, and his fumbling appeared to rob Win of her remaining anxiety. She seemed amused by his problems; her low chuckle raised the hair on his nape.

Finally, the door swung wide. "After you, my lady."

Win glanced at him with an odd expression, then timidly entered the foyer. The dower house furnishings were significantly simpler than the ducal residence, just one more reason Tristan liked the idea of living there. She swung round in a slow circle, admiring the high, molded ceiling.

If she asked for a tour, he'd be happy to oblige, but the curve of her throat demanded his attention. He locked the door behind him, captured Win against his chest, and swept his hands over nipples grown to hard points. "As much as I'd prefer a slow pleasuring," he murmured against her pale throat, "we should not dawdle today."

She curled an arm over her shoulder, capturing his head and holding him close to her. "That would be wise."

"Very wise." He tweaked her nipple, pressing his already hardened length against her bottom.

Winifred moaned and tugged on his hair.

The best way to make love, without creasing her gown beyond redemption, would be either to settle her on top, or have both of them standing. He glanced down and noticed the dust about the place had already marked Winifred's black widow's weeds. Standing would be best, until he had the place more thoroughly cleaned.

Impatiently, Tristan slipped her gown off one shoulder, freeing her full breast for his touch. She moaned as his hand filled with her flesh.

"Heavens, I missed that," she whispered. She wriggled her hips, and her bottom rubbed across his groin.

With a little maneuvering, he shuffled them to the staircase and positioned her so she could hold on. She clutched the newel post. He flipped up her gown, slid his hand over her thigh, between her legs, and into her damp curls.

"Sweetheart, I missed you," Tristan whispered. "You're so wet. So ready for me."

He nudged her legs wider with one foot, slipped the buttons free on his trousers, and roughly pushed them down. His cock ached to plunge deep immediately, yet he savored the slide of his length across the firm, white swells of her bottom until Win grumbled.

With one hand curled around her thigh, holding her open, and the other teasing her bud, Tristan breached her with one, smooth stroke. Win went up on her toes, holding the post so tightly her knuckles showed white. The intense heat and wet welcome made him take her hard, fast and with little mercy. He toyed with her until she sobbed and pushed back into his thrusts each time.

The slap of their bodies coming together, the desperate moans Win uttered, proved his ultimate distraction. With his release only moments away, he clutched her breast, plucked at her nipple mercilessly, until she tensed, then screamed the house down.

Lights sparkled before his eyes as his release shook him. He forced Win firmly against the staircase and he pumped his seed into her body, connected deeply to the woman he craved beyond breath. He'd never felt this way with other lovers. This primal, wild pleasure took his reason.

He pressed a kiss to her cheek as his world dipped and swayed at the image of making love to her each day. He liked that idea very much. Tristan dragged in a deep breath to settle his pounding heart. "Why haven't I seen a glimpse of you since Sunday? Have you been hiding from me?"

"My father keeps me busy." Win's gasping breaths reminded him he held her crushed against the stairs. He eased back, but stayed joined with her, unwilling to separate so soon.

"Hmm." He smoothed his palm over her breast. She moaned at his touch, a sound that pleased him immensely. "So responsive. Such limitless passion waiting to be set free." He slid his other hand into her damp curls, hoping she might be ready to make love again.

Win tensed. "I must return home soon, my lord," she whispered and tried to look over her shoulder. "Please, Tristan. Let me go."

She was right. They had to part, but he would make arrangements today to continue their affair. They were perfectly matched in passion. Tristan withdrew and eased her away from the staircase, supporting her as though she were fine china. Once she was steady, he quickly wiped his hand on his handkerchief, stuffed his cock back into his trousers, and straightened his attire.

When he glanced at his lover, he found her fidgeting with her gown. He moved to help, smoothing the fabric over her shoulder and breast, bending to brush the dust from the hem of the dark material. Clearly, she'd never had a man help her dress before. Her cheeks held a brighter flush than usual. It did seem more intimate than undressing, far more decadent than relations with his previous lovers. As he finished, Winifred kept her eyes downcast.

"What is it?" he whispered, pulling her

against his chest and pressing a light kiss to her lips.

She lifted her gaze to meet his. "I hadn't intended ..." She let the thought trail off.

"Neither had I. But it appears we cannot resist each other." He smoothed his hands over her back, puzzled by the urge simply to hold her. "I want to see you again. Often."

"I don't know."

"I do. I want you." He tipped her chin up and kissed her properly. No fast taking to dominate, but a slow possession designed to arouse and engage all her senses. He didn't have long to wait.

Win curled her fingers into his lapels and pulled him close. Within minutes, he was hard again. Painfully ready for more pleasure.

But he couldn't become so distracted he forgot what he wanted. Win had to agree to a more regular arrangement between them.

Reluctantly, he drew back. "Well, have I convinced you?"

She met his gaze with a passion-glazed stare. Slowly, she dipped her head in agreement.

Tristan wanted to leap about with relief, but he managed to subdue his reaction. "Excellent. We can meet here once I've moved in. I'm looking forward to christening my bed upstairs."

Win licked her lips, an action that wasn't wise if she wished to leave anytime soon. "When will that be?"

"Friday. The day you visit with my mother again." When her lips twisted into a grimace, he pulled her close. "Did my mother and aunts behave?"

"They were perfectly courteous."

"They're a menace." Tristan lifted her hand to his lips, kissed her palm, then tucked her arm through his. He guided her toward the locked door. "Next time, definitely a bed. And hours, not rushed minutes. I promise to make it up to you."

Winifred worried at her lip. "What about the servants? They will see me come here. The gossip will hurt my father."

Tristan unlocked the door and led her outside. "I have a plan for that. I won't ruin you to get what we both want. There will only be servants here in the morning, on loan from Staplehurst Hall. I've no need for them in the evenings, as I'll be dining at the Hall more often than not."

Her silence, as they crossed the yard, puzzled him. Most women he'd negotiated with had terms and rules they wanted followed. Apparently, Win's only concern was to hide their arrangement from society and her father. Tristan could indulge her whim to engage in a clandestine affair, although such secrecy was unnecessary. No one would look down upon the mistress of a future duke. Her father should be proud she'd risen so high.

"Are we in agreement, Win?"

She glanced up. "Yes, my lord."

Tristan needed one more kiss to last him 'til Friday. He cupped her face between his palms and captured her lips, ravenous all over again. Win held him tightly against her, and he reveled in the lust boiling between them. But he had to draw back, let her return to her usual life until the next time he could have her in his arms. She appeared dazed as he lifted her to the gig's hard bench, he wished he could drag her down again to finish what he'd started.

Behaving as a gentleman had never been so difficult.

He untied the horse, jumped into the gig, and set off at a fast clip so they reached the edge of town hopefully before her tardy return was noticed. That she was in a carriage with him, however, would not. Damn those meddling aunts for inviting her to tea today.

Justin had teased once too often about his brother's habit of visiting Davey's Lending Library within their aunts' hearing, and the next thing Tristan knew, Win was in the house downstairs taking tea with his mother. Although Tristan held Win in the highest regard, the inappropriateness of his mother taking tea with his mistress staggered him, and he had wanted to interrupt the tea and protect Win from her inquisition. But any action against the duchess would have only made the situation worse. He hoped she'd grow bored with Win's company before discovering their intimate connection. He didn't want his mother's temper to sideline the delicate negotiations with Win. Especially now that Win had agreed to see him again.

At the shop, he helped her down from the gig, releasing her as soon as she caught her footing. It was tempting to follow her and continue their conversation. He wanted to know what stones she'd prefer for her jewelry. He couldn't wait to see her wearing nothing but bright gems and silk stocking in his large bed. But he'd wait to hear her preference. He didn't believe she'd let him dictate everything between them. She was sure to have an opinion. He'd always been impressed she didn't resort to fluttering eyelashes or vapid giggles to catch a man's attention. All she need do was breathe, and his blood boiled.

After bidding her good day, Tristan swung up into the gig and set off for Staplehurst Hall. The slow drive cooled his blood until he had sufficient clarity to consider Friday's rendezvous. Although he had a lot to do, he couldn't help but smile. He almost had the delectable Winifred Moore as his mistress now. Country life couldn't get much better.

Except his mother awaited him in the front hall, tapping her toe impatiently. "A word, if you please." Her imperious tone brooked no refusal.

It would be nice to come home and not have the duchess accost him, for once. Moving to the dower house seemed too far away. She indicated for him to precede her, and, with considerable reluctance, he entered her sitting room. Thankfully, the aunts were absent.

"It's high time you married, Tristan. I want at least the possibility of grandchildren bouncing on my knee before next Christmas."

"Mother, is this to be a daily lecture?" He raked a hand through his hair. "I'll marry when I am good and ready."

The duchess scowled at him and sank into

her favorite chair. "I know my duty, and that is to promote a match that will see our line continue. With good planning, the right bride will provide comfort and pride for the family."

"Comfort!" Tristan exclaimed. "How is a wife supposed to keep a man happy?"

The duchess glanced down at her fingers. "Well, really, dear, a willing wife can be trained to meet your needs. Have you been engaged in intimate relations with no knowledge of the right way to go about it?"

Tristan threw his head back and roared with laughter. "Hardly."

She sniffed delicately. "You know there are several eligible young ladies in the district who would be perfect for the position of future duchess, all with the necessary pedigree to suit your needs. You just have to choose one and have the banns called. But do it before the babe arrives. I would prefer no irregularities for the succession."

It always amazed Tristan how far ahead his mother planned. A babe of his own would be years away. He'd not taken any chances, and...

He looked up, and his blood ran cold.

Dear God. What a fool he was. He'd not taken any precautions whatsoever with Win. He cursed under his breath at his thoughtless lack of control as his mother extolled the virtues of the local families. Win could be with child already, rushing head first into a scandal. It might be difficult, but he would have to remember to withdraw, or there were those other things mistresses used: sponges soaked in lemon, potions to expel the babe. He certainly wouldn't subject Win to the discomfort of a London Overcoat. But he doubted she understood how to prevent a pregnancy, so he would have to find out and explain it to her.

The idea of that discussion didn't sit well with him. Win's reluctance to continue their affair was already apparent. How would she react to the reminder that a child would bring scandal?

"Tristan!" His mother raised her voice in an obvious bid to capture his wandering attention.

Her lips moved, but he didn't register a word she spoke.

Win would make a wonderful mother someday, yet he couldn't marry someone of her common background, no matter how much he desired her or how responsive she was in the throes of passion. But a woman of good breeding, as ready for the marriage bed as Win, would suit him perfectly well. She and he could have a family together, a second life where passion, not duty, ruled. And later, he could make a marriage worthy of the duchy. One day. A long time from now. But not yet. "I'll consider the matter most carefully, Mother."

Meanwhile, he'd try to keep his head when Win was in his bed.

The duchess eyed him suspiciously. "Very well, just don't leave it too long."

CHAPTER SEVEN

AFTER WINIFRED HAD CALLED on the duchess for several weeks on a regular basis, the butler allowed her to find her own way toward the duchess's private sitting room while he re-settled his gouty leg. She wandered down the corridor, admiring the portraits of Tristan's ancestors lining the walls. Some of them were quite attractive. Some, like his great-grandmother, had kind eyes. But Tristan's great-grandfather—well, she'd consider that pointed nose quite a fright to kiss around.

"I tell you, she's ripe for the taking." Lord Justin's insistent voice came from behind a closed door to her left. Winifred stopped dead in her tracks as the sound of colliding billiard balls reached her. "Plumpest pair of assets about Town. Why, I'm sure she'd be perfect for you."

Knowing Tristan's brother had returned made Winifred uneasy. When he was home, he was something of a nuisance, calling at the lending library at all hours in search of his purported missing journal, attempting to charm her under her father's watchful eye. A pity the sight of him reminded her of Tristan and of how impatient she was for their next meeting.

"Really?" Tristan drawled. "Why do you think I'd be interested?"

"Well, come on, old fellow. You've been moldering here for the last month, and now you tell me you're still not returning to London. I think you must be ill."

"My health is excellent, Justin," Tristan replied. "I simply have no desire for Town just now."

Winifred smiled. She knew what he desired. Her. As often as they could arrange to meet. Tristan had charmed her into his bed and appeared in no hurry to push her out of it again. She rather liked the way he wanted her.

They had talked about their future together. Once.

He'd offered her jewels, gowns, pretty things, and an astonishingly large allowance to be his mistress. He'd wanted to take her to London for the rest of the season, to parade her on his arm at the theatre. All things she'd refused—immediately. Winifred would not leave her father.

Although Tristan often spoke as if they had years ahead of them, he'd sensibly never raised the subject of being his mistress again. But he'd spent an extraordinary amount of time and blunt in her father's shop, choosing books to expand the library at the dower house. His frequent visits gave them endless opportunities to talk about many varied matters. She quite liked his mind. He wasn't as frivolous as she'd first feared. He was interested in the ducal estate and commerce and was always on the hunt for books or opinions on improving management techniques. Her father had sold the viscount so many books, he no longer studied his shop ledger with a permanent frown.

"Have you settled into an arrangement with a woman in Devizes?" Lord Justin queried boldly. "Do tell, who is she?"

The clatter of pool cues alerted her that the game had ended. She took a quiet step forward, intent on hearing Tristan's answer. How did he regard her when they were apart?

"If I had, I'd hardly tell you the details, now would I? Discretion is called for when affairs are conducted so close to home."

"Well, I'd hate to dangle the carrot before the wrong woman during my visit and risk offending you."

"Believe me," Tristan replied, sounding sure of himself. "You'd have to dangle more than a few sparkly carrots before a woman of mine would cast me off for you."

"Oh ho." Justin chortled. "So there is someone. Now I have to find out who could entice you to remain here so long. She must be exceptionally talented between the sheets."

Am I talented in bed?

The reminder of their lovemaking, after being in Tristan's arms yesterday, sent her pulse racing. Was lust of this level natural? Normal? Was it becoming in a woman? Tristan seemed more than pleased by her responsiveness, except for the one time she'd been too impatient for the bedchamber and had encouraged him to make love on the hard staircase.

And referring to their trysts as making love was entirely Tristan's fault. That was how he labeled their frantic couplings.

Tristan's reply was muffled, as though he moved deeper into the chamber.

Disappointed not to hear his words, Winifred crept beyond the door, closer to the dragon's den. Not that Her Grace was a dragon, precisely. But she would be waiting with her sisters at her side. Winifred had to remain on her guard. They had welcomed her into their ranks with open arms, quite a frightening prospect, considering what she frequently did with Her Grace's son on the way home from tea.

So far, not by any word or look, did Winifred feel discovered.

The duchess had declared, as a widow, Winifred would be a suitable addition to her country circle. If not for the estrangement between her parents and their families, the noble lines from which she descended, made her inclusion possible. However, Winifred had never sought to use her lineage to elevate herself. In fact, she rarely mentioned her pedigree at all. She might be a duke's granddaughter, but she hoped the duchess included her for her company alone.

Tristan, however, had viewed his mother's frequent invitations with wary concern and urged her to be cautious.

The sound of the duchess's voice yanked Winifred from her musings. "Ah, there you are, my dear. I had begun to fear you had been waylaid."

"No, Your Grace." Winifred smiled

warmly. She liked Tristan's mother, despite the threat of discovery and the duchess's probable reaction to the scandal that discovery would cause. "Perhaps I walked a touch slower today. The grounds are very fine."

The duchess preened and drew Winifred into the chair next to hers. Today's topic was her next ball. Her Grace was engrossed in the planning, and, within a few minutes, Winifred had been conscripted to be the duchess's right hand in organizing the event. That could mean daily visits to the duchess and more opportunities to see Tristan in secret.

When Her Grace excused herself to attend her husband's summons, Lady Armitage encouraged Winifred to take a turn about the grounds with her, since Lady Herriot already napped in her chair.

"I find the grounds of Staplehurst Hall lovely this time of year," the countess exclaimed as they crossed the lawn.

"Yes," Winifred said, tucking her hands behind her back as they paced along the green path. "The summers are wonderful."

"Yes, the grounds about the house are lovely, but I am also fond of the wilder parts of the estate. I quite often find myself strolling toward the dower house to admire the flowers in the afternoon. Ramsbury has repaired the neglected garden quite admirably."

Winifred's heart squeezed tight. Had the countess discovered Winifred meeting with the viscount? Overheard them? She had to be careful not to betray herself. "I'm sure they are quite lovely."

The countess linked arms and kept walking. "You should know since you visit the dower house often enough to meet my nephew in secret."

Winifred's heart slammed into her throat. Although her heart fought her plans, she had to remain calm. There had always been a danger this day would come. Tristan was a fool not to have considered the possibility, or perhaps such discoveries were everyday events for him.

For a moment, Winifred feared she might die of mortification. She pressed her damp palm to her waist to contain her anxiety.

The countess must have noticed her distress because she pushed Winifred to a stone bench as soon as they came upon one. "Don't lie to me about this. Are you with child yet?"

Winifred didn't look up. Despite discussing methods of conception, neither she nor Tristan managed to keep their heads at all times. There had been quite a few notable slips where it had not been till later that preventing a pregnancy even occurred to her. "I don't know, my lady. It is possible though."

The older woman clucked her tongue. "Most young ladies would have landed my nephew in the muck by now and demanded he marry her. Why haven't you?"

She shrugged. "It's not a pleasant experience being forced into marriage. I don't want that."

The countess turned her back and stared off in the direction of Staplehurst Hall. "Because of my affection for your late mother, I will take a part in rescuing you from my nephew's unthinking ways. A future duke's bastard can be either an asset or a liability. Ramsbury's child will be the former. When you are certain, and if my nephew fails to behave as he should, you are to come to me—not the duchess. This unfortunate development will greatly distress her. I have a little used house in Gloucestershire standing empty but for a few faithful servants. It was part of my dowry. You will spend your confinement in seclusion. And after the birth, you may either return to your father, or stay with the child. You cannot bring Ramsbury's bastard back here under any circumstances. I will not have my sister embarrassed."

Winifred gulped at both the offer and what her future entailed. Either exile with her child, or return without. She couldn't bear to part with a child she and Tristan had created.

But for the moment, all was speculation. Her courses were only a little late.

"Are we in agreement?" the countess asked.

Winifred raised her gaze to the older woman's face for the first time, expecting to see scorn. Anger. Instead, the woman appeared anguished over Winifred's potential situation.

"Yes." She agreed reluctantly. Although her condition was not confirmed, there might still be a chance she would need the countess's generosity to spare her father shame. One day, probably soon, Tristan would tire of her and return to London. But his child would need protection from poverty. She hadn't considered this at the start of the affair when she'd turned down his offer of jewels and a pension. A life lived in exile seemed a small price to pay for her utter stupidity, and staying here would bring unhappiness to those she cared for most. Besides, if she left, no one would see her broken heart.

"Now, if you are ready, we should return to

the Hall. I see my sister is waiting for us on the terrace."

Winifred stood and smoothed her dark skirts, quite hating the sight of them. "I am ready."

The countess fell into step, but her unhappy sigh reached Winifred's ears. "I had such high hopes for you, my dear. You have fitted in well with the duchess, and she has come to regard you as a potential daughter-in-law, although her son refuses to discuss the succession with her. If only he would make that wish a reality. But I fear he might simply be sowing his oats. I am so sorry for that. For all of your drab mourning, I should have realized he'd see your seduction as a challenge, and I should have taken it upon myself to protect you. I don't suppose he's given you any indication of deeper affections?"

Tristan appeared to enjoy their time together, but aside from once asking her to become his mistress, he had never offered to change their arrangement into a permanent state. Not to the kind for which the duchess had apparently hoped. For all the joy Winifred found in his arms, he'd never given her cause to expect more. "No, my lady."

"Well, we have an agreement." The

countess pursed her lips as if she'd bitten into sour lemons. "I'll stand by you no matter what becomes of this tragedy."

Winifred nodded, already wishing the parting of ways with Tristan was over so she could grieve over what might have been. It may not have started out as more than lust but she loved him so deeply, so passionately. She couldn't imagine not seeing him again. Her legs felt like lead, her smile for the duchess painted, and she took her leave as soon as courtesy allowed, without diverting to meet with Tristan. The memory of Lady Armitage's sad gaze stayed with her every step of the way home. The lonely bite of the coming winter chased her on the wind.

A sharp tug at his cravat didn't settle Tristan's nerves. Neither did slipping on his coat with the help of his valet. He was dressed for the day, dressed to ride until his scheduled meeting with Win in a few hours. Yet he was strangely uncomfortable.

Something bothered her.

Of late, their conversations had grown stilted, their passion a touch desperate, and the urge to discover what she withheld overpowered him.

Perhaps her unexpected trip to visit a friend he'd never heard mentioned before caused the growing distance between them. According to Win, she had much to do, and she had only grudgingly agreed upon their rendezvous today.

He had not liked her hesitation.

The slow pace of country life required relief in the delicious form of Winifred Moore. Tristan found it hard to imagine a greater contentment to be found in these parts. Knowing his lover was as eager to see him as he was her made him impatient to greet each new day. He looked forward to winter, when he could build a roaring fire and make love to her on the deep hearth rug.

However, when winter did come, she'd freeze solid on the walk over from the village, if she managed to visit him at all.

He dug his fingers into his waistcoat pocket and removed what he'd hidden there. Gold chain looped over his fingers as he pulled his gift from his inner pocket. The small pendant, something for Win to remember him by during her month-long absence, had burned a hole in his pocket since he'd purchased it. She would scowl at him for breaking her rule. He'd never had a lover who hadn't accepted small tokens of affection. But Win claimed they felt too much like payment for services. A distinction he hadn't considered she might make or deem important enough to fight about. So he resisted the urge to spoil her, buying only this one gift when he'd learned she'd be going away.

He hadn't realized she had friends beyond Devizes.

In truth, her life beyond their afternoon trysts remained a mystery. She shared little beyond the present and rarely spoke of her connections. Her friend was simply her friend. He didn't remember if Win had even mentioned the woman's name.

The thin, gold chain held a diamond, not large enough to appear vulgar, but perfect for his passionate woman. His woman. His lover. His daily need. Somehow, he'd managed to lay eyes upon her every day, though he doubted she realized how many excuses he'd used to place himself in her path. His obsession hadn't frightened him. On the contrary, he found the idea of spending his life with one woman vastly appealing. He'd grown tired of hiding their arrangement.

"Are you going out already?" Justin inquired from the door.

Tristan tucked the necklace into his pocket before his brother noticed the trinket and questioned him. "Directly after breakfast. I was on my way down. What are you doing here?"

"Mother mentioned you're always in the saddle early these days. Wonderful. I'll join you for breakfast, and then we can be on our way."

Tristan rolled his eyes, but made his way to the door, then down the long flights of stairs to his breakfast room, his thoughts still focused on how to see Win during the colder season. Sending a carriage to collect her would be out of the question. The whole of Devizes's society would notice that arrangement.

His brother plunked his heaped plate on the table. "Are you going into town or riding about the estate today?"

"The estate. Why? Are you worried the townsfolk will see us together and conclude we've patched up our supposed differences? My poor, neglected, younger brother," Tristan murmured. "People are beginning to believe me an ogre."

His brother grinned impishly. "That rumor garnered me significant sympathy with the ladies. Even the elusive Mrs. Moore shed a tear for me over your callous disregard for my tender feelings."

Tristan snorted. "I doubt that. Mrs. Moore has greater sense than to indulge in such theatrics."

Justin scowled. "And how have you become an expert on Mrs. Moore's senses? From what I've seen, she barely spares you a glance."

Tristan gritted his teeth. He'd inadvertently stumbled into another conversation about Win he didn't want to have. Justin was convinced Tristan had a lover here at home and tried to determine her identity at every opportunity. So far, he'd managed to fool his brother, but Tristan wished Justin would leave well enough alone.

"As I said, Mrs. Moore has excellent sense." Better a lie than the truth. But the truth would burst from his tongue if he weren't careful. He wanted Win with a powerful ache. Knowing she'd be beyond his reach soon didn't help his temper. "Better to keep up your charade of the poor neglected brother. I understand Miss Wheaton has been a great comfort to you. She fluttered her eyelashes at you quite prettily yesterday morning over your depressed spirits. Be careful there, brother. She is aiming to catch an unwary man in the parson's noose."

"She did not flutter her lashes," Justin growled, and then his face glowed with excitement. "You were not there to see that. Who told you?"

Caught in his own war of words, Tristan struggled to find an alternative source for that particularly funny piece of gossip. Win had told him, of course. She'd been close to hysterics during the telling too, but Tristan shouldn't have known anything about that encounter. "I heard a rumor to that effect."

Justin squinted at him. "That happened outside Davey's Lending Library. I had called in to speak to Mrs. Moore about my missing journal when the Wheaton chit bailed me up outside—inquiring after you, by the way. I'm fairly sure Mrs. Moore would have noticed. Why would she tell you?"

Tristan shoveled a forkful of steak into his mouth and chewed slowly before answering. "Your conceit is astounding. Mr. Davey stood behind his counter. Men gossip too, or are you dazzled by every false smile that crosses a woman's face?"

"Mrs. Moore was happy to see me."

Tristan's breakfast, what he'd managed to

consume, settled like lead in his belly. "Tell me, brother, did you manage to acquire that garter from Mrs. Moore? I believe you indicated you'd have it in a week. That was what, three months ago now?"

Justin's face lit a fiery red. "Did you tell her of my plan? I bet that's why she's turned so cold."

"Really, Justin, why would I bother? Win's clearly not interested in you, or you'd have that garter fluttering for the whole world to see." Tristan stood and dropped his napkin to the table, prepared to leave early just to cover Justin in his dust. He could not afford to return late to meet Win. Not today.

"Win! That's it, isn't it? You've made Winifred Moore your country mistress," his brother crowed loudly. "You cunning devil. She must have quite a few tricks hidden under that black gown to keep you here panting after her month after month."

Tristan spun on his heel, stalked back to the table, and slammed his fist into his brother's face. Justin hit the ground hard and didn't get up. He lay still, staring at Tristan in stunned surprise. A trail of blood seeped from his lip.

Winifred wasn't his mistress, never had been contracted to be his mistress, and he'd be damned if he'd let anyone label her a doxy. She was far more important to him than that.

"Repeat that to anyone, and I'll finish you," Tristan growled. "Don't be here when I get back." He turned on his heel again, ignoring Justin's plaintive wailings, and escaped the house.

All he needed to spoil everything was Justin's loose tongue repeating his discovery.

When Justin returned to the Hall, Tristan knew his brother would find a way to garner sympathy over his injuries. He just hoped Justin had enough sense to lie about the cause. His brother might even find a caring woman in town to nurse him back to health. But Justin wouldn't show that face to Win anytime soon. She was leaving, and for the first and only time, Tristan was glad of it because he had lost his dispassionate edge where Winifred Moore was concerned.

CHAPTER EIGHT

WINIFRED ROSE from the vast bed and tugged Tristan's shirt over her head. The long, soft linen fell to her knees in a decadent wash of sandalwood. She dragged in a deep breath and settled a hand over her belly. Now that she no longer had Tristan's hands, lips or eyes on her, she noticed her stomach rumbled uneasily again. The distracting sensation reminded Winifred of her final incentive for this trip—escape from the result of this scandalous affair.

Tristan rested on his back, exhausted from their stolen hours in the dower house. She couldn't hold back her pleased smile. He was a perfect lover. Tender, demanding, and extremely thorough. But his thorough loving these past months had caused her considerable distress.

She was with child, her belly soon to burst

beyond her power to keep the condition secret. Although ruin lay beyond discovery, she wouldn't change one moment of her time with him. As she had feared, she'd made the foolish mistake of falling in love. She was certain now and she ached with grief over what she had to give up.

But as Tristan had never indicated he felt the same, she had few options.

"What are you staring at so intently?" The bed ropes groaned as Tristan moved about. "Not the patchy walls again? They're to be repapered next week with the pattern you like. When you get back, it will all be done."

"No, not the walls, I was thinking about my visit to my friend," Winifred lied. "I have so much to do before I go."

Tristan slid off the bed. "I still don't understand why you have to go." He pulled on his trousers and poured himself a drink. "The woman has three grown children of her own to assist her in her time of need."

Winifred's fictional friend did have three fictional children, but the need was all Winifred's. She needed to disappear discreetly from Devizes's society. She hadn't even told the duchess of her hastily arranged trip. She glanced over at Tristan, hoping he might make some sort of declaration. "It is nice to be needed."

Tristan held her gaze. "I need you too."

She couldn't hide her surprise, but when he didn't offer more, she made herself laugh it off. "I doubt you'll be lonely for long. Mrs. Deets has been watching you quite closely. You will only have to crook your finger to find a replacement to warm your bed."

"She can watch me." Tristan swooped on her and dragged her against his chest. "I'll be watching for your return."

Sometimes the viscount said the sweetest things. But Winifred had learned tender words between lovers held little meaning beyond the bedchamber. He just wanted to convince her to let him under her skirts again. Even now, barely minutes since their last loving, his eyes glowed with hunger. His desire pressed at her expanding belly.

The realization that he'd never meet their child caused her eyes to fill with tears. He'd make a good father one day, when he was ready to produce his heir. She hoped he managed to marry for love and not simply for the woman's connections. More than anything, she wanted one of them to be happy with their life.

Hoping to avoid further questioning about

her trip, Winifred kissed him. She slid her tongue into his mouth, dueled for supremacy, and lost the battle, as always. Tristan liked to control, but he often teased her with the possibility of victory. The bitter taste of brandy on his tongue would be one of the last memories she had of him.

Winifred curled her arms about his bare shoulders. She loved the way he effortlessly lifted her from the ground, supporting her tightly against him. He pushed aside the shirt she wore, cupping her bottom, teasing her lower lips with his fingers. He would be the last lover she would ever have. Was it wrong to want a few more moments with the man she loved to distraction?

She tightened her legs about his waist and encouraged him to claim her.

Winifred kept her eyes closed, savoring sensations that would have to last her a lifetime. His skin slicked under her fingers; his breath was a hot pant at her throat. Tears pricked her eyes as they strained toward completion. She was so close to bursting she pressed her head to his shoulder to hide her distress. Her release came upon her, and she squeezed her eyes shut. But the tears wouldn't stop.

Tristan's thrusts became frantic; her spine

slammed painfully against the wall he'd pushed her against as he filled her body with the last of him she'd ever have. At least the pain would help explain the tears. Tristan's concerned gaze met her watery one.

"Oh, Win, I'm so sorry," he whispered. He smoothed her hair out of her face, then lightly brushed her spine. "I don't know what came over me."

"It's all right," she said, forcing a smile to her lips to erase the frown on his. "It was just the passion of the moment. I doubt I've suffered serious hurt."

"That doesn't give me the right to treat you so callously."

Winifred slid her fingers into his hair and held their heads together. "I don't mind when you're so passionate. Sometimes it excites me too."

She could swear his eyes glazed over at her pronouncement. By tomorrow, he'd have dreamed up a new position in which to make love. Yet she wouldn't be here tomorrow.

Tristan brushed a light kiss to her cheek. "Did I ever tell you how lucky I am that you chose me for your lover?"

Rather than answer, she shook her head.

Her eyes stung with unshed tears. But she couldn't let them fall now.

"The luckiest man in England." He gave her a brief, tight squeeze. "Don't stay away too long."

Winifred dropped to the ground on shaky legs. Would he miss her? Her heart soared with hope at the idea their afternoons had become more about companionship and less about slaking their needs. She struggled not to cry. This was the last time she'd see him. She couldn't fall apart yet. When she was on the road to Gloucestershire and to her new life, she'd give in to her tears and fall apart.

With Tristan's help, she dressed, the process slowed by his need to kiss her skin. Eventually, she was respectable enough to be seen, although Tristan's efforts in assisting with her hair today left a little to be desired.

With a pang of regret, she glanced around the chamber they'd loved in these past months. Tristan had freed her hungers to alarming depths. He'd brought them out until she hardly recognized herself.

"It's time for me to go," she whispered.

Tristan made no move to stop her. She picked up her bonnet, tied the ribbon beneath her chin, and faced the bedchamber door.

"Win?" Tristan called as her hand fell on the latch. "I'll miss you."

Those three little words pierced her heart. Somehow, she found the strength not to turn, not to run back into his arms and confess the real reason she had to leave. It was better Tristan be unaware of the scandal of an illegitimate child and live out his life in ignorance.

She opened the door and walked out.

Winifred descended to the lending library with a sigh. She'd made it home yesterday without falling apart, made it through the night without sobbing her heart out. But now, she needed to keep up her charade of contentment long enough to fool her father for one last meal before she caught the stage.

Her father sat at his cluttered worktable. New books towered about him at dangerous angles; a glass and a half-empty bottle of whiskey sat at his elbow. "I forgot to ask, how were the ladies yesterday? Was your visit a pleasant one?"

Winifred put the cork back in the bottle and tucked it into the cupboard out of his reach. "Yes, of course. They are in excellent health." The same lie she told every week. She did call on the ladies, but not as often as she led him to believe. It was something of a miracle her deception had remained undetected.

"Good, good," he replied distractedly, with one hand curled around the daily newssheet, while he lifted the glass to his lips for a long sip with the other.

"Is there something distressing in the paper, Papa?"

He slid his glass and the paper onto the table. "Yes, it seems the duke has died. My father. I'm trying to decide if I should go and pay my respects to my family."

Winifred clutched at his arm. "Oh, Papa, I'm so sorry. I know how much you missed them, despite all they did to you."

"We dishonored both our families, and our betrothed's families, by acting on our love." He pressed a kiss to her forehead. "But I wouldn't change the past. Your mother and I were happier together than apart."

Winifred had a sneaking suspicion she'd believe the same of herself later. Her life was richer—better—for having shared Tristan's bed. But it didn't matter. Her lover would never change the status quo. "I remember."

Her father folded the paper neatly and

tucked it between the tottering piles. "She never complained, you know. About the loss of her status, or about our fall from the upper ten thousand. Her father warned me that she would never adjust. A duke's daughter deserved a better life, he told me."

"So did a duke's son. They should never have disowned you both." Winifred hugged her father, thinking how different her life might have been if she'd grown up in privilege. The acknowledged granddaughter of two dukes should have lived a charmed existence. But if she had lived life within the bosom of the *ton*, she might never have known the real Tristan and found the love of her life in him. "Will you go and see your brother now?"

He scratched his jaw. "I don't know. My elder brother has known my location these past years. If Max had wanted to see us again, then he would have sent word or arranged to meet after our father's ire had cooled. Perhaps it's best if I stay away. Leave things as they are, so to speak. We've done all right without them."

"You're right." Winifred wrapped her arms tightly about him and squeezed. "We are better off without them. Well, whatever happens, I want no part of them."

"You sound like your mother." Her father

chuckled deep in his throat. "My Adelade had fire too. Once she decided to flaunt convention, there was no stopping her from having me. I didn't stand a ghost of a chance."

Although it pleased her to know she had a similar temperament to her mother, Winifred wasn't as brave. She had to leave today, before the babe in her belly began to show and caused considerable harm to her father's standing. Better he never learn of her disgrace. But she would miss him terribly in the months ahead.

Despite the tears that again threatened to fall, she gazed into his familiar, lined face. "I sense you still want to go."

"The trip would take days on the stage, and my welcome would be uncertain." He gave her a wry grin and tapped her cheek. "How can I go? I must earn my living."

Winifred pressed a quick kiss to his cheek. "My leaving is poorly timed, isn't it?"

Her father peered at her intently. "It's good of you to care so much for your friend in her time of need, but again, you speak as if you are leaving forever. You'll be back once Mrs. Landry's confinement is over, won't you?"

"Of course, Papa." Winifred turned away, dismayed she'd given him cause to suspect her of subterfuge. "Now, if you'll excuse me, I still have chores to do." Winifred hurried to the kitchen, but her father followed and perched at the end of the table. Under his constant gaze, she prepared their breakfast, cleaned up the dirty dishes, and put everything away again. "Mrs. Clemens said she'd take care of you."

"Mrs. Clemens is a fine woman, but she'll never be able to make your potted mutton to my satisfaction." He heaved a dramatic sigh. "When you return, I'll expect to see it served every night of the first week."

Despite her sadness, Winifred managed a laugh. "After a week, it won't be your favorite anymore, Papa. Are you sure you want that?"

"I'll never tire of your potted mutton!" he exclaimed fervently, eyes twinkling with amusement. "I'll go up and collect your trunk."

Winifred summoned a smile. "Thank you."

Once he shuffled out, she sagged against the kitchen table and wiped the back of her hand across her clammy brow. The pregnancy had turned her stomach to choppy waters at the scent of certain foods. Even Papa's favorite potted mutton unsettled her.

It would be nice not to pretend to feel well anymore. Lady Armitage had arranged for a knowledgeable woman to attend her in Gloucestershire, one who could answer her questions about the coming birth. If they got along well, the countess had promised to engage her services until well after the child arrived. And Lady Armitage said she would do her best to witness the birth too. She promised to write a letter for the child to prove its parentage.

And when the time came, the countess would inform Tristan of his bastard's existence and spare Win the embarrassment.

CHAPTER NINE

TRISTAN'S MOTHER HUFFED. "Really, must we go? You know I never cared for him after his dreadful treatment of Charles."

At the end of the breakfast table, hidden behind a newspaper and a well-stocked plate, Tristan's father did his best to ignore his wife. "We should put in an appearance," the duke replied sternly.

Beside Tristan, his brother, Justin, and Aunt Armitage nodded in agreement.

Why had he come here this morning to listen to his parents bicker?

The reason was obvious, of course—to keep from dwelling on Win's departure. After a restless night and early morning stroll to the back garden of the lending library in the hope of spotting her, Tristan needed some serious diversion. Watching the tense war that was his parents' marriage should do the trick, as well as his brother attempting to keep the peace between them.

This was his future. To marry for the power gained from an alliance. To marry with the barest hope of returned affection or regard. He didn't hold out for love; he'd already found love with Win. Knowing that Win claim his heart was as natural as breathing now, though he'd never told her how important she'd become to him.

Tristan set his silver to the table and glanced about him. He should have told her yesterday, or the day before, or at any time in the weeks before that. He was discontent among the finery of his childhood home. He'd come to value the simplicity of the dower house and knowing Win would be with him there. Yet it wasn't enough. He couldn't see her enough.

Little by little, Win had taken over his life. She moved things when he wasn't looking. She'd made the house a home, and he couldn't imagine sharing the space with anyone else. Proper wife be dammed. Money be damned. His parents be damned.

He wanted only Win. He wanted to marry her.

But could they survive? Could he support Win as he wanted if his father cut him off?

"But." He felt his mother's gaze land upon him and he looked up. "Tristan should stay here and manage things in our absence."

At that, his parents had his full attention. "What are you speaking of, Mother?"

"Why, the funeral, of course." She tapped the paper at her elbow. "The Duke of Bristol has died, and your father insists we pay our respects. It is simply the worst time to travel."

The duchess glanced anxiously between Tristan and his brother. Justin's lip had darkened to an ugly purple, and he scowled to match. Tristan wouldn't apologize. Win's honor had to be championed.

"His Grace does have the right of it, Dezzie," his aunt Armitage piped up. Her gaze fell on Tristan, and as it did quite frequently of late, disgust lingered in her expression. He had no idea what he'd done to displease the countess—it couldn't be Justin's battered state because that scowl had fallen on him repeatedly over the past month.

The duke snapped his paper closed and threw it at a footman. "The scandal is long since over. Surely, you can forget it all."

"They treated Charles and Adelade shockingly," the duchess railed. "Their own flesh and blood disowned and tossed aside. If not for your generosity, I shudder to consider what would have happened to them."

"Charles wasn't quite as poor as all that," his aunt piped up again. "He had planned out the elopement ahead of time. Thank goodness."

"Yes, it all turned out well in the end, but it could have all gone terribly wrong. What if our father hadn't agreed to Armitage marrying you after you helped Adelade escape her parents' watchful eye? They attempted to destroy your reputation, sister."

"Armitage is a forgiving man, Dezzie. He never held me accountable for it all. Not when the scandal threw me in his way."

Tristan raised his hand to stop the flow of chatter. He was totally confused. Who were his parents and aunt defending so valiantly? "Mother, who are you speaking of?"

"Why, Mr. Davey, of course." His mother wrinkled her brow. "Your aunt, Lady Armitage, was engaged to him once but he eloped with Adelade instead."

"Why would Lady Armitage be engaged to marry a common bookseller?"

The look the duchess cast over him made him feel an imbecile. "Charles Davey is the third son of the late Duke of Bristol, of course. Why, I remember so clearly the night we learned that Charles and Adelade had defied their parents and run off to Gretna Green to marry." The duchess sighed somewhat dramatically. "A love match if ever there was one. It was the talk of Town for a decade."

At the head of the table, the duke huffed. "Damn fool was too proud to ask for assistance until your mother browbeat him into coming here. Wouldn't take the dower house either, had to sully his hands in trade."

Tristan's stomach lurched, and then fell. "Is Winifred Moore related to the Duke of Bristol?"

"And the Duke of Newbury too. Adelade was his youngest. Fine girl. Fine families, except for their pig-headed obstinacy. She's the only granddaughter on both sides, if memory serves." The duchess chuckled. "Her blood is probably bluer than yours, Tristan, even if she's not acknowledged. But of course this should come as no surprise to you. We discussed her bloodline at length during the summer."

Tristan put down his fork and glanced at his aunt and brother to check that he wasn't dreaming.

Justin's eyes widened, but his aunt Armitage had covered her mouth with her hand.

"No, Mother, I believe I missed that essential conversation."

The sisters exchanged a long look before the duchess clucked her tongue. "Well, really. You only had to look it up in the Peerage. I let you have your head knowing there'd be a wedding in the end. What have you been playing at these past months?"

Tristan couldn't answer that. He and Win did talk, albeit between bouts of frantic lovemaking, but he'd never considered Winifred's connections seriously. He could marry her without his parents raising a fuss.

He could have his passionate Win to wife and wake beside her each morning, something he'd longed for since that first night. He'd watch her grow large with his child. His child. He wondered how long it would take to fill her belly.

And then the truth hit him square in his gut.

Win left today on a pilgrimage to care for a distant friend, so distant her response to his questions about her return had been vague, if she'd answered him at all. Was she leaving now to hide the fact she was already carrying his child?

The more he considered their involvement, the more certain he became.

She'd never told him they couldn't tumble into his bed because of her woman's time. Not once. He counted back in his head to the day their affair started months ago.

Why hadn't he noticed she never refused him? Why the hell hadn't she said something?

But she'd never asked him for a damn thing in return for his affections.

Affections? Tristan chuckled. He was damn well utterly, foolishly in love with her and hadn't ever told her. No wonder she was leaving him.

He glanced at his mother and aunt, noticing the way Lady Armitage appeared to swoon. As she pressed her head into a shaking hand, Tristan realized she'd had a hand in Win's departure. "I am an utter fool."

His mother clucked her tongue again. "Yes, dear. Why don't you take a trip into town and visit the lending library?"

Tristan shook his head, watching as the countess gulped. "Not the shop. Win leaves today."

"I'll have your horse saddled." Justin escaped from the room through the open terrace doors.

Tristan threw his napkin down, captured his aunt by the arm, and dragged her with him into the front hall. "We will speak in a moment." He spotted the butler advancing but waved him away. He then turned on his aunt. "Now. What have you done?"

"Nothing but see that Winifred is cared for properly. You never proposed, and she's beside herself with worry that the duchess will discover she's carrying your bastard."

Tristan gritted his teeth. He'd never proposed marriage, but he'd always planned to be part of Win's future. If he'd paid attention and actually listened to his mother, they might already be wedded by now. Good God, could one kick one's own backside? Could Win forgive him for treating her so dishonorably? "The visit to this so-called friend can wait. I believe I'll be taking care of Win from now on. What exactly has she agreed to have happen?"

Lady Armitage leaned against the wall. "She will travel to Wren Cottage, my property in Gloucestershire, and remain in seclusion until her expectation arrives."

When she fell silent, he shook her arm. "And after that?"

His aunt licked her lips. "She said she wouldn't be coming back. She couldn't bear to hurt her father with the news of her disgrace."

Win was leaving because of the child. That's what she wouldn't say this past month.

"Damn it to hell." Tristan raked his hands through his hair. Panic assailed him. "Go away, Aunt. Get out of my sight."

Lady Armitage wisely scurried for the sanctuary of the rear parlor, but his mother caught up with him while he paced the front steps.

"What do you mean, leaving? She can't leave—she loves you. We have a wedding to plan."

Although his mother had married for the title, for greater influence in society, she extolled the virtue of love matches. Her uncanny knack of spotting true, bone-deep affection had never been known to fail her. As Tristan glanced down into his mother's worried face, it became clear to him she didn't know about Win's pregnancy. At least something had slipped her notice—one less mistake she could rail at him for. "She's not going anywhere."

"Good." She indignantly set her hands to her hips. "I've never known women to act rationally about the men they love. But I've noticed they do tend to forgive easily enough, once the right words are spoken."

Tristan squeezed her arm. Were there enough words in existence to explain his stupidity? Well, he'd spend the rest of his lifetime proclaiming his devotion to make amends to his dearest Win.

Justin rushed up with a horse. "You used to tell me everything, Tris," he muttered, gaze darting to where the duchess stood. "Why didn't you tell me you loved her? I would have let her be."

Tristan grasped the reins and set a foot in the stirrup. "Would you tell me if a woman owned your heart?"

His brother scowled. "Not bloody likely."

"Exactly." Tristan vaulted into the saddle. "But I should have told Win. Long ago. Wish me luck."

"Happy hunting."

Tristan kicked the horse to a gallop. With luck, the stage hadn't arrived. But he'd be cutting it bloody close. If she'd already gone, he'd follow her all the way to Gloucestershire.

The long drive blurred beneath him, the outlying tenant buildings falling behind in his dust. But the township was crowded with people. The stage stood waiting.

Recklessly, Tristan raced through the street and brought his mount to a skidding stop before he collided with the carriage team.

"Hold," he shouted to the driver.

The burly coachman snarled. "The stage holds for no man or beast. Get away from there."

"Winifred!" Tristan roared, uncaring for the scandal he could cause. "Winifred Moore, get out of that damned stage!"

Voices shrieked in outrage around him as the coachman pulled a club from beneath his bench, obviously intending to move Tristan by brute force. But Tristan wouldn't go anywhere without Win.

Her face appeared at a window briefly. "Oh very well."

Muttered curses tumbled from the open door as the passengers expelled her. The rough treatment angered him, but he breathed easy when she stood on solid ground again.

"Now can we be on our way?" The coachman yelled. "You have your wife."

His gaze fell on Win, flushed but defiant. "That I do." Tristan dismounted and moved his horse out of the way. The coachmen tossed a trunk at Win's feet, and after much noise and swearing, the coach rattled away.

But the townsfolk lined the streets, watching them.

Tristan walked forward and caught Win's hand in his. "Mrs. Moore."

"My lord." Although she smiled, she tried to tug her hand back.

Tristan raised her fingers to his lips and pressed an ardent kiss to her knuckles.

"I missed something important, Mrs. Moore."

"A book, perhaps?" Her gaze skittered about the growing crowd. "My father would be only to happy to help you."

She wouldn't like a scandal; she wouldn't like everyone to know how close they'd become, but he could, and would, do the honorable thing. Gaining her forgiveness, however, might take time. He tucked her arm through his and began to walk up the street.

"It's amusing you should mention books. Apparently, I should pay more attention to my study of the Peerage. It's amazing where a man might stumble upon a duke's relation, a grand-daughter, perhaps, and take advantage of the amazing opportunity."

Win gazed at him with complete distrust. "You dragged me off the stage to tell me something of no possible importance."

Tristan came to a halt before the steps of the village church, took her hands in his, and pressed them against his panicked heart. "Well, when you will one day become a duke, connections by marriage are deemed somewhat important to your family."

Winifred's face turned a fiery red. She was angry, and he couldn't blame her. "Is that so? Arrogant and rude connections matter to you?"

Tristan squeezed her fingers, noticing that a crowd of familiar faces had followed them along the street. "Oh, yes but not entirely. You see, no matter how well connected a granddaughter might be, it is important that the lady's character, her passions, her very nature be well-matched to the gentleman too. However, said well-connected lady would have to be a saint to forgive such a self-absorbed scoundrel. Or, if he's very lucky, she's madly in love with him and failed to mention it, as he did. Perhaps she will forgive the idiot one day for making her worry about her future, but he is prepared to do penance at her feet for the rest of his life for a chance to regain her respect. And her hand in marriage."

When Win's mouth dropped open he kissed her hand again. "Win, I've always been told that love is for those without a duty to fulfill. However, when even a foolish man finds those two perfect necessities blended into one fair lady, he would be blind and stupid not to take advantage. I was very stupid until this morning, my love."

Win's eyes widened. "Stupid?"

"I love you so much I cannot bear for you to go away."

Winifred closed her eyes briefly, and when they reopened, tears glittered in the familiar, dark depths. "If you hope to gain any advantage from offering marriage to me, you will be sorely disappointed. My father and mother were disowned by their families. I have no desire to become better acquainted with their relations."

"I would never demand it of you. Your connections merely smooth the way to gain my father's approval of the match." Tristan dropped to his knee in the dirt. "But do marry me, Winifred Moore. I don't care if you make me suffer for being such a fool, but you've had my heart from the first, and I adore you."

"Oh," she whispered. Tears fell from her eyes, and after a long moment of silence he tugged on her fingers to remind her that he still waited for her answer.

Win dipped her head the slightest inch, so Tristan rose to pull her into his arms. The crowd around them roared to life, and he caught sight of her father, standing in shock beside his mother and her two grinning sisters. How they had made it here from Staplehurst Hall so fast escaped him. But he was glad they had pushed him, each in their own way, to choose the perfect woman for his wife.

He nuzzled Win's ear. "Tell me true, beloved, have I done all that I can to begin to fill our nursery?"

Winifred gasped and buried her face into his cravat. "The babe comes next spring."

"Excellent." Tristan's heart burst with happiness. He took a deep, calming breath and met his Aunt Armitage's weeping gaze. He dipped his head, acknowledging her efforts to protect his Win from his stupidity. He wanted no bad blood between them to mar his happiness.

"Well, I might be slightly tardy in my proposal, but at least we appear to be well ahead of mother's schedule for next Christmas. She's demanded a babe to bounce on her knee for next year's celebrations." Tristan hugged her tightly. "If the child is a girl, I'd like to call her after our mothers and your sister. How about Felicity Adelade Jane Greene? That has a nice ring to it. And for a boy, Charles Stephen Tristan. Do those names please you?"

"You've already considered names?" Liquid-dark eyes met his, accusation simmering in their depths. "How long have you known about our child?"

He rubbed his hands over her back to calm her. "Only since this morning, but the image of you with our child in your arms has plagued me for some time. I've done my fair share of daydreaming about a life with you. The one I wasn't brave enough to seize without a push."

She scrubbed at her cheeks. "I feared you'd be disappointed to lose your freedom."

Tristan cradled her face between his hands, relieved she belonged with him now and forever. He wanted everyone to know how deeply he cared. "Win, I've never been as free as when I am with you. I've hated every moment we were apart."

Despite the tears streaming down her face, she sought his lips to seal their fate and their future. And it was not like their first kiss, nor the second, nor the last.

It was better.

The End

DISTINGUISHED ROGUES SERIES

Chills ∼ Broken ∼ Charity

An Accidental Affair ∼ Keepsake

An Improper Proposal ∼ Reason to Wed

The Trouble with Love ∼ Married by Moonlight

Lord of Sin ∼ The Duke's Heart

Romancing the Earl

One Enchanted Christmas

Desire by Design ∼ His Perfect Bride

Pleasures of the Night ∼ Silver Bells

Seduced in Secret ∼ Yours Until Dawn

SCANDALOUS BRIDES

Wicked with Him

Desperately Seeking Seduction

Love and Other Disasters

WILD RANDALLS SERIES

Engaging the Enemy ~ Forsaking the Prize

Guarding the Spoils ~ Hunting the Hero

*

SAINTS AND SINNERS SERIES

The Duke and I ~ A Gentleman's Vow

An Earl of Her Own ~ The Lady Tamed

*

REBEL HEARTS SERIES

The Wedding Affair ~ An Affair of Honor

The Christmas Affair ~ An Affair so Right

*

MISS MAYHEM SERIES

Miss Watson's First Scandal

Miss George's Second Chance

Miss Radley's Third Dare

Miss Merton's Last Hope

ABOUT THE AUTHOR

USA Today Bestselling Author Heather Boyd believes every character she creates deserves their own happily-ever-after—no matter how much trouble she puts them through. With that goal in mind, she writes steamy romances that skirt the boundaries of propriety to keep readers enthralled until the wee hours of the morning. Heather has published over fifty regency romance novels and shorter works full of daring seductions and distinguished rogues. She lives north of Sydney, Australia, with her trio of rogues and a four-legged overlord.

Learn more about Heather at:
Heather-Boyd.com

THE RISE OF THE GREAT OLD ONE

JASMINE JARVIS

Available from Black Hare Press

SHORT READS

WARDENCLYFFE by GREGG CUNNINGHAM
HADES 11 by PAUL WARMERDAM
BLOOD AND SILK by ZOEY XOLTON
AS ABOVE, SO BENEATH by JOSHUA D. TAYLOR
THE RISE OF THE GREAT OLD ONE by JASMINE JARVIS
DEAD MAN WALKING by DAVID GREEN
CHRYSALIS by KIMBERLY REI
MOUNT TERROR by E.L. GILES
HELL HATH NO FURY by CHISTO HEALY
THE RECKONING by STEPHANIE SCISSOM

UNDERGROUND

MIRACLE GROWTH by TIM MENDEES
THE RETURN by GABRIELLA BALCOM
UNDERGROUND by S. GEPP
WHISPERS IN THE DARK by K.B. ELIJAH
SWIRLING DARKNESS by SAM M. PHILLIPS
THE GATE TO THE UNDERWORLD by E.L. GILES
COLD AS HELL by NEEN COHEN
THOSE OF THE LIGHT by NICOLA CURRIE
TIME'S ABYSS by JAMES PYLES
UNDERWORLD GAMES by JONATHAN D. STIFFY
PLACE OF CAVES by CHARLOTTE O'FARRELL
AFTER THE FALL by STEPHEN HERCZEG
BEYOND HUMAN by MATHEW CLARKE
THE FALL OF PACIFICA by M. SYDNOR JR.